NIGHTMARE ACADEMY
CHARLIE'S MONSTERS

5TH RING

4TH RING

3RD RING

2ND RING

1ST RING

SECRETS OF THE NETHER

KNOWN GREMLIN
INFESTATION

HAGS OF
THE VOID

TROUT OF TRUTH

NETHERFORGE

HYDRA CAVE
(RUMOURED)

BT GRAVEYARD

INNER CIRCLE

First published in paperback in Great Britain by HarperCollins
Children's Books 2008
HarperCollins *Children's Books* is a division of
HarperCollins*Publishers* Ltd
77-85 Fulham Palace Road, Hammersmith,
London W6 8JB

The HarperCollins *Children's Books*
website address is:

www.harpercollinschildrensbooks.co.uk

1

ISBN-13: 978-0-00-727370-6
ISBN-10: 0-00-727370-3

Dean Lorey asserts the moral right to be identified
as the author of the work.

Printed and bound in Australia by Griffin Press

NIGHTMARE ACADEMY
CHARLIE'S MONSTERS

DEAN LOREY

For more ferocious monster fun log on to
www.nightmareacademy.co.uk

HarperCollins *Children's Books*

DEAN LOREY HAS WRITTEN EXTENSIVELY FOR
TELEVISION AND MOVIES. THIS IS HIS FIRST BOOK
FOR CHILDREN. HE HOPES IT WILL KEEP YOU
UP ALL NIGHT.

For my wife, Elizabeth,

and our sons, Chris and Alex.

I love you guys.

PART ONE
THE NIGHTMARE DIVISION

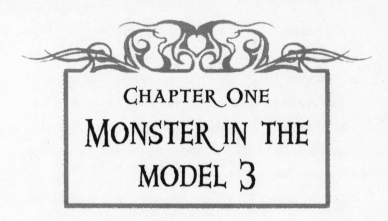

CHAPTER ONE
MONSTER IN THE MODEL 3

O N MOST DAYS, Charlie Benjamin was pretty sure he was the loneliest kid on planet Earth. He went to school by himself in his home on a quiet street inside a gated community. Although the houses all looked nearly alike on the outside, there were several different models a buyer could choose from.

The Benjamins lived in a model 3.

"The model 3 is the superior model," Charlie's father frequently told him. He was an exact man with the exacting name of Barrington. "The 1s are obviously prototypes – less said about the 1s, the better. The 2s, however, are what happens when you rework something too quickly. You often take *two* steps backwards to take one step forwards. Which brings us to the 3s – the simple, solid, *dependable* 3s."

The model 3 was Charlie Benjamin's prison.

At thirteen, he was short for his age, with unruly, sandy-coloured hair, dark brown eyes and a spray of freckles across his nose and cheeks. His elbows and knees were remarkably unscabbed and he had virtually no bruises, thanks to his well-meaning mother's insistence that he stay inside the house.

"It's an uncertain world," she often told him. "I can protect you in here, but once you step outside..." This was always followed by a grave shake of the head, as if the horrors of life outside the model 3 were too painful to contemplate.

"I know you keep saying that," Charlie said to her one Saturday morning after a particularly grave shake of the head. "But that doesn't make it *true*. I'm tired of being stuck here all the time. I want to go to normal school."

"*Normal* school?" his mother replied. "Honey, we have everything a normal school has right here. Books and computers, papers and pencils, tests and marks..."

"But no students," Charlie interrupted. "I mean, other than me."

"That's true," his mother agreed pleasantly. She was such a pleasant woman, in fact, that she'd never even blamed her own mother for naming her Olga. "And *thank goodness*, because no students means no teasing, no bullying, no making fun of you just because you're a little bit different."

Even though Charlie was the first to admit that he was *more* than a little bit different, protecting him from the abuse of other kids by locking him away in the house seemed a little to him like removing a splinter by chopping off his hand – it got the job done, but at what cost?

The price is just too high, he thought as he heard the postman shove the morning post through a chute in the front door. With a sigh, he walked over to retrieve the usual assortment of bills and catalogues – always for his parents, never for him. And that was when, to his astonishment, he spotted a small blue envelope addressed to "Charlie Benjamin".

"That's me," he gasped.

Almost in a daze, Charlie opened the envelope, to reveal an invitation to a party – and not just any party. It was a *sleepover* party at the home of some kids who lived just down the street. Charlie didn't know them personally, of course – he didn't know any kids his own age – but clearly someone there had taken pity on the small, strange boy who lived in the model 3.

Charlie read the invitation twice to make sure it really said what he thought it said; then he read it once more for good measure. Once he was satisfied that he wasn't dreaming the whole thing, he showed it to his parents.

"Absolutely not," his father said after glancing at the invitation.

"But *why*?" Charlie immediately shot back. "I've been good. I've done all my schoolwork – in fact, I just finished the chapter on geography."

"Honey, what your father means," his mother said, "is that we certainly wish you *could* go, but what if you have one of your 'nightmares'?"

One of his nightmares.

Even though it had been years since Charlie had had a catastrophic nightmare in public, the thought of it happening again made him absolutely weak with dread. And yet – here was an actual, *real* opportunity to make a friend.

He couldn't pass it up.

So he begged his parents. He pleaded. He offered to do the dishes for a year and mow the lawn and learn French. He argued that it had been so long since his last unspeakable nightmare that he had surely outgrown them. Finally, he told his parents that going to the sleepover party was the only present he wanted for Christmas and his birthday *combined*.

For the next two years.

Three if that's what it took.

After much arguing behind closed doors, his parents finally relented. Which is how, later that night, Charlie found himself skipping up the steps of a stranger's house with an overnight bag slung over his shoulder.

"You know how to get hold of us if utter disaster occurs?" Charlie's mother asked nervously, following behind him.

"Yes, Mum, I know how to use a *phone*."

"Do you want me to quickly review any of the *fus* I've taught you – *kung* or otherwise?" his father offered.

"I'm not gonna need to fight anyone with *kung fu*, Dad. Nothing's gonna happen, trust me."

"We never should have permitted this," his mother moaned. "And a *sleepover* no less! What were we *thinking*?"

"Nothing will go wrong," Charlie said, looking longingly at the other boys inside the house. They were clearly already having a blast. "I won't have any nightmares tonight – *trust me*."

"Of *course* we do, son," Mr Benjamin replied as he handed Charlie a mobile phone. "We know nothing will go wrong, but just in case it *does*, I put our home number on speed dial so you can call quickly if something absolutely catastrophic occurs."

"Thanks, Dad," Charlie said resignedly, taking the phone from him.

"And if you look in your backpack," his mother added, "you'll find earplugs in a little bag. You can use them if the other children tease you and call you horrible names."

"OK, Mum," Charlie said, wishing desperately that they would leave – but they just stood there.

"Well!" Mr Benjamin said finally. "I guess we had better go. We love you, son, and we trust you and we feel certain in our hearts and in our souls that nothing cataclysmic or disastrous will happen this evening."

"It won't," Charlie said. "Everything will be fine. I *promise*."

And everything *was* fine... for a while. Charlie played computer games, ate pizza and watched PG-13 horror movies. Incredibly, he even found himself on the verge of making a friend – a tall, blond kid everyone called "FT", which, Charlie learned, was short for "FTW", which was short for "For the Win", because of his terrific video-game prowess.

It was the most fun Charlie had ever had in his entire life.

Then it was time to go to sleep.

Accounts differed as to what exactly *happened* during

what newspaper headlines would soon call "Terror at the Sleepover Apocalypse", but certain facts were not in dispute. At some point, around three in the morning, tremendous screaming and crashing came from the bedroom where the kids were sleeping. When the adults in the house finally managed to fling open the door, they found all of the children suspended from the ceiling, wrapped tightly in cocoons of extraordinarily tough webbing. The only child not encased and suspended from the ceiling was Charlie, who stared at the shattered bedroom window in shock.

"My God, what *happened*?" gasped the father when he saw his children dangling like Christmas tree ornaments.

"A giant spider," Charlie said, and pointed to the broken window. "It left through there. It's not my fault."

No one blamed Charlie exactly. After all, how could a thirteen-year-old kid have done such an extraordinary thing to so many other children? And yet even the local newspaper reporter wondered why Charlie was the only one left unharmed by the "giant spider" – a fact that Charlie himself had puzzled over. Even though no one actually accused him of anything, after the kids were cut down and revived, none of them would speak to him or even look at him – not even FT. Charlie had gone to sleep that night thinking he'd finally made a friend but he'd woken up to find himself the object of fear and panic.

It wasn't the first time.

In fact, from almost the moment he was born, sleep and Charlie Benjamin were an explosive combination. The very first public disaster had happened during naptime at Welcoming Arms nursery school.

Charlie was three years old.

Even though he couldn't quite recall the specifics of the nightmare he'd had while he and the rest of the children slept on mats inside the darkened classroom, he could vividly remember the inhuman howling and shrieking that had snapped him out of it. As the nursery school teachers raced in to see what could possibly be making such astonishing noise, little Charlie woke, to find the classroom around him utterly destroyed.

The colourful nursery-rhyme wallpaper hung from the wall in ribbons, as if slashed by talons. The fish tank lay shattered against an overturned bookshelf as the fish inside frantically flipped and gasped for air. A spray of glass from the back window glittered brilliantly across an easel, which lay splintered on the floor.

"What happened?" the teacher asked, her face ashen.

"I'm sorry," little Charlie replied, shaking. "I didn't mean to do it."

"*You* did all this?" the teacher asked incredulously.

Charlie nodded. "Sometimes bad things happen when I have nightmares."

The pattern was always the same.

He would go to sleep at home in his soft, warm bed and everything would *seem* to be fine – at least for a while. But sometime during the night, terrible snorts and growls would rip through the house. By the time his parents burst into his bedroom to see what was wrong, the place would be ruined – mattress stuffing tossed everywhere, carpet torn, glass shattered. And even though they never actually caught him in the process of destroying a room while in the grip of a bad dream, they figured he *must* be doing it – it was the only explanation that made any sense. In fact, Charlie dreaded going to sleep because he was terrified about what he might find when he *woke up*.

The incident at naptime (later dubbed the "Naptime Catastrophe") quickly became legend, and it wasn't long before the other kids starting chanting "Nightmare Charlie" at him whenever he walked by. Soon, his parents were summoned before the nursery school administrator, who carefully explained that Welcoming Arms would no longer be welcoming Charlie.

"The other children are *afraid* of him, you see," the administrator said with terrible seriousness. "In fact, they refuse to take their naps when he's in the room. This is absolutely unacceptable. Naptime is the cornerstone of the nursery school experience. It is the glue that holds the remainder of the curriculum together. Without naptime, chaos is inevitable and ruin is sure to follow!"

"I can sense your passion," Charlie's father agreed in his calmest voice. "But if you think that Charlie is the *cause* of their distress—"

"He's not," Charlie's mother snapped as she gently rubbed her son's back with her warm, strong hands. "The other children have been teasing and tormenting *him* – not the other way around. My heavens, do you know what they call him? 'Nightmare Charlie'!"

"Quite right," Barrington continued. "But my point is that perhaps Charlie could be moved to a different area of the classroom while the rest of the children are sleeping."

The administrator was horrified. "We cannot go down that slippery slope. If I make one exception for one boy, pretty soon I'll be making two exceptions for two boys, and, before you know it, it's all exceptions and no 'ceptions' if you get my drift." He shook his head sadly. "No, Welcoming Arms and 'Nightmare Charlie' – I mean, *Charlie* – must now go their separate ways."

Even though Welcoming Arms was the very first nursery school to kick Charlie out, it certainly wasn't the last – Balance Point, Happy Child, Li'l Learners and

Perfect PlayPals followed soon after. But that's where Charlie's horrible streak of getting kicked out of nursery school finally came to an end, because by then, he was old enough to get kicked out of primary school.

Charlie was six years old.

"I know you claim there's nothing wrong with him," the headteacher of Paul Revere Elementary purred to Charlie's parents, slurring through adult braces. They were a rat's nest of decaying food – an archaeological dig that contained everything he had eaten in the previous week. "But our school psychologist believes he suffers from a variety of serious problems. *Very* serious. In fact, he has diagnosed Charlie with – let me see..." Mr Krup began reading from a file. "Yes, here it is. OCADMMD."

"That's an awful lot of letters for such a little boy," Mr Benjamin said, putting his arm protectively around Charlie's narrow shoulders.

"And he's earned every one of them, believe me! It stands for Obsessive-Compulsive Attention Deficit Mental Meltdown Disorder." Mr Krup set the file down and glared at Charlie, unearthing an ancient piece of sweetcorn that lay trapped against a molar. "Now, being a state school, we are required by law to give him an education. However, we think it is in 'Nightmare Charlie's' – I mean, *Charlie's* – best interests to be removed from the general population and sequestered in a trailer off school grounds, where he can only associate with other children that have been diagnosed with as many letters as he has. Sign here, please."

The headteacher slid a form over to Charlie's parents.

Charlie's mother slid it back.

"No," she said.

"Pardon me?"

"You and the other children may not like Charlie, Mr Krup. You may not *understand* him. But he is a wonder. And if you can't see that, then you don't deserve him. He will leave with us today and never return." Olga stood and smiled triumphantly. "Until I can find a school that sticks, I will teach him myself."

And that's just what she did.

For the next seven years, Charlie went to school in the protective bubble of the model 3 – until that bubble burst on the night of the Sleepover Apocalypse.

Why am I such a freak? Charlie thought as he sat on his couch and stared out of the large front window of their home, hoping to catch a glimpse of the neighbourhood kids as they got out of school. Even if he couldn't play with them, he figured he could at least *watch* them. It had been five days since the Sleepover Apocalypse, and he was still reeling.

At the end of the block, the school bus from General MacArthur Middle School groaned to a shuddery halt. Its door accordioned open and students poured out, chomping gum, hauling bulging backpacks, laughing and playfully shoving one another. Charlie quickly spotted FT, who removed a frisbee from his book bag and whipped it towards one of the other kids.

Charlie waved to him. FT saw him in the window and shot him an icy glare; then he turned back to the other kids, ignoring Charlie completely.

"Do you think they'll ever stop blaming me?" Charlie asked his mother. "About them hanging from the ceiling in cocoons, I mean."

He knew the answer was *no*, but, to his amazement, his mother simply shrugged, barely looking up from the afternoon soap on the TV. She had changed so much in the last day or so that he hardly even recognised her. She seemed to be completely uninterested in him, which wasn't like her at all. Charlie hoped that she was simply coming down with the flu, because he couldn't bear the thought that his recent disaster might have caused her to finally, after believing in him for all these years, just *give up*.

"I want to go to school next year. *Normal* school," Charlie said to his parents during dinner that night.

"Charlie, we've gone over this and over this," Barrington replied. "Do I have to remind you about the Sleepover Apocalypse?"

"But that wasn't my fault!" Charlie shouted. "Everyone keeps blaming me, but I told you I didn't do anything to those kids – it was a giant spider! I actually *saw* it that time!"

"Charlie, *please*," Mr Benjamin said, massaging his temples. "This conversation's over."

"It is *not* over! I can't have any of my nightmares at school because it's during the day, so why shouldn't I be able to go like everyone else?"

"*Because they'll hurt you!*" Mr Benjamin shot back. Instantly, he looked as though he regretted it. "You may not have one of your nightmares, but it won't matter. They've already labelled you, Charlie. You're *different*... and they'll torture you for it. They always do. Now please, go and get ready for bed, son."

"I don't want to. I—"

"*Charlie.*" Barrington's voice was a stone door, slamming shut.

Charlie got up from the table and stormed out.

Mr Benjamin sighed heavily and turned to his silent

wife. "The older he gets, the harder it is to keep him here. I know we do it for his own protection, but, much as it pains me to say it, someday soon we're going to have to let him face the world on his own."

Olga turned away without saying a word.

"Are you all right, dear? You're not coming down with something, are you?"

She shook her head. Mr Benjamin took her hand gently in his.

"I know, I don't want to let him go either. It's cruel outside the model 3, and a boy like Charlie, a wonderful, *unusual* boy, well..." He shook his head sadly. "He's going to take *such* a beating."

The glow-in-the-dark stars glued on to the ceiling above Charlie's bed had grown faint. The walls of his room were covered in soft foam. There was no glass in there, nothing sharp or heavy that could potentially hurt him if thrown or broken during a particularly destructive nightmare – only rounded corners, thick padding and windows made of safety plastic. To Charlie, it sometimes felt like an insane asylum designed to protect him from himself, from the horrible things that often happened after he fell asleep.

And sleep, as usual, was slow in coming.

He tried to empty his mind of the crazy thoughts that were zinging around his brain by writing two new entries in the "Wicked Awesome Gadget Journal" he kept beside his bed. The first one (gadget number 47) was an idea for a "Wicked Awesome Laser Watch" that emitted a beam of light powerful enough to temporarily blind bad guys, giving you time to get away. The second one (gadget number 48) was a handheld device that used a complicated computer chip to identify smells for people who had lost their noses in horrible accidents. He called it the "Wicked Awesome Odorometer".

He had no idea how he could actually build any of the objects he dreamed up, but that wasn't really the point – the important thing for now was the *idea*.

A squirrel nibbled at a nut on his windowsill. In fact, he could hear more of them in the attic above, scratching away softly. It was oddly soothing.

Without even realising it, Charlie finally fell asleep.

It started out as a good dream. He was playing frisbee with a group of kids on the school playground – in fact, they were the same ones from the Sleepover Apocalypse, but they didn't seem frightened of him now. FT threw the frisbee to Charlie, but an unexpected gust of wind caught it and took it far down the field. Charlie sprinted across the freshly mown grass with blinding speed. He leaped over a soccer goal and, spinning in mid-air, managed to snag the frisbee in spectacular fashion.

"That's the best catch I've ever seen!" FT said.

"It just comes natural to me, I guess," Charlie replied, trying his best to appear casual.

"Would you like to have a Slurpee with us?" another kid asked, pointing to a Slurpee machine that stood gleaming at the edge of the field. "Nothing tastes better on a hot day than a cold Slurpee with your friends."

"Sounds great," Charlie said, and followed the kids over.

The Slurpee machine glowed with an inner brilliance. FT turned the handle and poured an icy red drink into a styrofoam cup.

"This one's for me," he said. "Now your turn. Do you want red or blue?"

"Red," Charlie said. "Same as you."

FT placed a fresh cup under the tap and turned the handle. Nothing came out. "That's strange," he said. "Maybe something's stuck in there." He put his finger deep inside and searched for a blockage.

"Find anything?" Charlie asked.

"Not yet," FT said. "Wait a minute... My finger's stuck."

He tried to pull it out, but it wouldn't budge. As he struggled, a cold wind whipped down from the darkening sky. Thunderheads rolled in.

"Maybe someone should go and get help," Charlie said, turning to the other kids. He was surprised to discover they were gone. In fact, *everyone* was gone now – everyone but Charlie and the trapped boy.

That's weird, Charlie thought.

Suddenly, the tap on the Slurpee machine turned on and the machine hummed back to life. The frozen red drink flowed from the machine, through FT's finger and into his body, filling him like a balloon.

"Do something!" he yelled. "It hurts!"

Charlie tried to turn the handle, but it wouldn't budge. The kid's face began to swell as his colour changed – pink, then red...

"It's so *cold*," FT moaned, shivering. "Help me!"

"I'm trying!" Charlie shouted back, but there didn't seem to be anything he *could* do. The boy's face bloated grotesquely, expanding like a balloon animal, as his skin turned from a deep red to a dark shade of purple, the colour of a rotten plum. The wind that whipped down from the sky was freezing now and Charlie could see his breath on it.

Somehow it had become night-time.

He looked upwards and saw stars... but they looked too perfect. They had five distinct points and were glowing faintly. Suddenly, Charlie realised that they were the stars on the ceiling of his bedroom. When he looked down, he was shocked to discover that he was now back *in* his bedroom – along with the thing that FT had become.

It looked something like a scorpion – slick, purple-black skin stretched tightly over a bloated body full to bursting with juices. Sharp claws clattered at the end of long, unnaturally thin arms. A skeletal tail with a thirty-centimetre-long stinger wavered dangerously above its head and the tongue that flickered, snakelike, in and out of its horned snout gleamed metallic silver.

Charlie tried to shout, to scream out for help, to do *anything*, but his mouth had gone as dry as chalk and the beating of his heart filled his ears like mortar fire. As the creature neared him, Charlie reached over, took the pencil off the bedside table next to his Gadget Journal and, summoning all his courage, jabbed the pencil into his hand while yelling, "Wake up!"

Charlie woke from his nightmare with a shout. Sweat matted his hair to his forehead and his heart pounded in his chest so hard, he felt it might break his ribs.

"I'll never go to sleep again," he said as he slid out of bed and carefully felt his way across the dark room towards the thin, comforting line of light underneath the door that led to the hallway.

His hand touched something.

The creature from his nightmare stood there.

"No," Charlie gasped.

Towering over him, it raised its long, curved stinger, preparing to strike. A thick, poisonous-looking fluid oozed from the tip. Charlie's knees went watery and he dropped to the ground.

"Don't," he said.

The monster's tail whistled furiously down towards him with the force of a sledgehammer.

At exactly the same moment, the window beside Charlie exploded inwards as a tall man crashed through. He made a movement with his arm so fast that it looked almost as if time skipped forwards a beat. A blinding flash of blue light snapped in front of Charlie like a lightning bolt. It snaked around the creature's stinger, causing it to arc off course just enough to spike harmlessly into the floorboard, spraying Charlie with splinters of wood.

The stranger landed with a thud, grabbed Charlie by the front of his shirt and yanked him to his feet, away from the monster. To Charlie, he looked just like a cowboy

– dusty blue jeans covered the tops of his oiled leather boots, a worn cowboy hat rested on his wide brow and in his right hand he held a lasso that glowed with an electric blue fire. Charlie suddenly realised that it was actually the *lasso* that was wrapped around the creature's stinger.

"Howdy, kid," the cowboy said with a crooked grin. "Nice to meet you finally. Looks like I showed up just in time."

CHAPTER TWO
A CLASS-5 SILVERTONGUE IN FULL VOICE

"**W**HO ARE YOU?" Charlie asked, staring in shock at the stranger in his bedroom.

"Name's Rex," the cowboy answered. "I'm sure you got a ton of questions, and I'll get to 'em in just a bit – assuming we live through this, of course. Things are about to get ugly."

"Uglier than *this*?" Charlie replied, gesturing to the monster in his bedroom as it frantically tried to free its stinger from the floorboards.

Rex laughed. "Just you wait. You're gonna get *nostalgic* for this moment once that old Silvertongue starts singing."

"Singing?" Charlie repeated, confused.

Suddenly, that's just what it did. The creature opened its mouth and stuck out its abnormally long silver tongue, which twisted and vibrated like a tuning fork. No words came out, only notes, but they were sweet as spun silver and amazing in their intricacy.

"Ah, no," Rex moaned, then turned to the window and shouted, "Where's my portal, Tabitha darlin'?!"

"Working on it!" a female voice answered, and Charlie spun round to see a pretty woman with short red hair scrambling through the shattered window. She wore long trousers, as green as her emerald eyes, and her fingers and neck glittered with an extraordinary amount of jewellery.

"There's my sparkly queen," Rex said. "You're a sight for sore eyes, sweetness."

"*Don't* call me 'sweetness'," she shot back as she strode towards him.

"Sure thing, sugar lips," he replied with a grin.

Clearly aggravated, Tabitha gritted her teeth and extended her right hand. Brilliant purple flames began to dance over her body, charging the air with electricity. Charlie felt the hairs on his arms and legs stand on end. The creature continued singing – faster now, more intense – and Charlie was awestruck by the alien beauty of its voice.

"It's incredible," he murmured.

"Yeah, right up until it crescendoes," Rex said. "Then it's gonna get bad, fast."

"What happens then?"

"Oh, our heads'll explode."

"Our heads will explode?" Charlie gasped.

"It's actually quite an interesting phenomenon," another voice chimed in. Charlie spun back towards the window to see a short, sweaty man with a neatly trimmed beard trying to climb over the jagged plastic. He wore a dark, three-piece woollen suit – far too hot on this warm night. "You see," the man continued, wiping sweat from the tip of his long nose as he grunted with effort, "the precise frequency of the Silvertongue's final note – *stupid window* – causes the air inside a human's sinus cavity to vibrate at such a high speed that it literally shatters the skull. It's a very effective attack strategy."

"Gee, you think?" Rex said.

"Yes, I *do* think, unlike you," the bearded man shot back, still struggling with the window. "And may I remind you that you are not to take any action without prior approval from me. You know the rules."

"You still talkin', Pinch? I drifted off for a second."

"I *hate* when you call me that," the man called Pinch moaned.

"And I hate wasting my time arguing with a weasel like you, especially when I got a Class-5 Silvertongue in full voice to worry about."

"It's a Class-4," Pinch said, falling into the room with a thud.

"It's a 5!" Rex snapped. "Count the dang spikes on its tail – or can't you count?"

Charlie looked at the spikes on the creature's tail. "Yup, there's five," he confirmed.

"See, Pinch – even the *kid* knows."

Suddenly, with a squeal like a rusty nail being prised from a plank, the still-singing Silvertongue wrenched its stinger free from the floorboards. The glistening tail slipped out of the lasso and attacked Rex, who leaped backwards as it whistled past his face.

"How about that portal, princess?" Rex shouted.

"It's coming," Tabitha yelled back.

"That's comforting," Rex said, dodging another poisonous tail lash with the grace of a matador. He pulled a short sword (which also glowed with a blue fire) from his belt and used it to parry the swordlike stinger.

The creature's singing had now become a shimmery blur of sound. Charlie could feel his entire head vibrating like a paint mixer. His eyes felt like they were going to pop out of his skull.

"Do something!" Pinch begged. "It's crescendoing!"

"What's going on in there?" someone suddenly shouted from the hallway. "Charlie, are you OK?"

"That's my dad," Charlie said, grimacing. "I'm not supposed to be out of bed."

Just then, Tabitha's entire body was engulfed in purple fire. There was a blast of hot air and a large portal, like a doorway, opened in the centre of the room. It was circular and big enough to drive a car through. Its edges burned with purple flames, just like the ones that danced across the woman.

Rex smiled. "That's my girl."

The bedroom door flew open and Mr Benjamin rushed in. "Charlie, are you having another one of your nightma—" He stopped cold and stared in shock. "Er, what's this all about?"

The Silvertongue glanced towards him.

That was all the diversion Rex needed. He threw himself at the monster and the force of his weight sent it reeling backwards, interrupting its final, deadly note. The creature stumbled into the portal and dropped out of sight. Charlie ran forwards to see where it went.

What he saw shocked him.

The portal seemed to hover high in the air above a bizarre alien landscape. Far below, a tangled mass of mustard-coloured crystals snaked through one another like barbed wire. The Silvertongue crashed down into them, snapping some crystals and getting sliced by the razor-sharp sides of others. Soon it was gone from view, lost in the deadly thicket.

"Wow!" Charlie exclaimed, staring in awe.

Rex jumped to his feet and slipped the short sword back into his belt. "And that's how we do *that*," he said with a cocky grin. "Sometimes I amaze even myse—"

Suddenly, with a hideous screech, a giant, crimson-coloured bat plummeted out of the red alien sky and flew through the still-open portal. It snatched Rex in its gnarled claws and, with a fury of flapping wings, yanked him backwards through the gateway and into the strange world beyond.

"Rex!" Tabitha screamed.

Almost instantly, Rex's lasso arrowed back out of the portal, missing Charlie's cheek by centimetres. With a sharp *crack*, it snapped around the bedroom doorknob and pulled tight. Rex held on to the other end, jerking wildly in the air like a kite in a hurricane as the huge bat-like creature struggled to fly off with him.

"Pull!" Rex yelled. "Pull and *don't let go*!"

Tabitha and Charlie grabbed hold of the lasso and played a desperate game of tug-of-war with the bat as Pinch paced fretfully. "I *told* him he needed prior approval for any actions," he moaned. "And now we are in a *situation*."

"Dig in!" Rex shouted as the bat leaped and dived like a sailfish on a fishing line. "And Pinch – *shut up*!"

"Sticks and stones," Pinch said, then turned to Charlie's father. "Mr Benjamin, do you, by chance, have any flour in the house?"

"Flowers?"

"No, sir. Not flowers, as in daisies and petunias, *flour*, as in the sentence 'I need flour to bake my pumpkin pie'."

"Oh," Barrington said. "I think so."

"Get it, please," Pinch replied. "With some urgency, if you don't mind."

"Right away," Barrington said, running out of the room.

The batlike creature flapped furiously, its wings thundering with a sound like a freight train as it slowly dragged Charlie and Tabitha towards the open portal.

"Help us!" Tabitha shouted to Pinch. "It's pulling us into the Nether!"

Charlie looked down through the portal and saw the razor-sharp crystals far below, waiting to spear them if they fell through.

"Technically speaking," Pinch replied, "I'm only here in a management and advisory capacity."

"*Just help us!*" Charlie, Rex and Tabitha screamed simultaneously.

"Oh, very well," Pinch said, and grabbed the lasso. With his added strength, they began to pull Rex back towards the bedroom as Barrington ran in with a bag of flour.

"Got it," he said, panting.

"Excellent," Pinch replied. "Now throw it on the Netherbat."

"The what?"

"The Netherbat!" Rex roared. "The only giant bat around here that's trying to kill me!"

"Oh," Barrington said. Just as Charlie, Pinch and Tabitha pulled the creature through the open portal and into the bedroom, Mr Benjamin ripped open the bag, unleashing a snowstorm of flour. The Netherbat's wings whipped the powder into a frenzy, and soon everything in the room was coated in a thick cloud of fine white particles. Almost instantly, the Netherbat dropped to the ground and stumbled forwards as if drunk.

"What's happening?" Charlie asked.

"Netherbats, like regular bats, use a form of sonar called echolocation in order to *see*," Pinch replied. "The fine grains of flour clog its transmitters, effectively rendering it blind."

"Thanks, Mr Science," Rex said, elbowing the creature hard in the head. It released him, still coughing and gasping. With one quick, fluid motion, Rex loosed the lasso from the doorknob and cracked it like a lion tamer, herding the creature back towards the open portal. The Netherbat stumbled blindly through the gateway and tumbled down, spinning crazily, until it was finally speared on one of the needle-like crystal spires far below.

"Close the portal," Rex said.

Tabitha waved her hand and the purple, fiery-rimmed gateway slammed shut. There was silence all around them then as the flour settled, blanketing everything and everyone in a peaceful white shroud – in a crazy way, it reminded Charlie of Christmas.

"What in the world is going on here?" Mr Benjamin finally managed. "Who *are* you people?"

"Name's Rex," the cowboy said as he snatched Mr Benjamin's hand and shook it firmly. "Nice to meet you. I'm a Wrangler."

"The proper term is *Banisher*," Pinch sniffed.

"Proper, but lame. I'll stick with Wrangler. This here's Tabitha." He gestured to the woman. "She's a Portal Jockey."

"We prefer to be called Nethermancers."

"As you can see, she's got a terrific crush on me."

"I do not!"

"Oh, really?" Rex replied with a grin. "How's the

weather over there in Denial City? Hot and bothered?"

"You're unbelievable," Tabitha said, shaking her head.

"I kind of am, aren't I?" Rex replied.

"Just ignore them," Pinch said, turning to Mr Benjamin. "My name is Edward Pinch. I am what we call the *Facilitator* of the group, and I am the responsible party."

"Responsible for *what*?" Rex asked.

"For saving your life," Pinch shot back.

"Ah, you didn't save my life. I was about to tell Mr Benjamin here to go and get a bag of flour. You just beat me to it."

"Your arrogance is *astonishing*," Pinch said. "I'm not looking for you to do a backflip in my honour – a simple thank you will be sufficient."

"All right then," Rex said. "Thank you, Pinch, for fixing what the princess screwed up."

"What *I* screwed up?" Tabitha shot back.

"That's right," Rex replied, turning to her. "You opened that portal all the way into the 5th ring, didn't you?"

"Of course," she said, "because we were banishing a Class-5 Silvertongue. Class 5s are supposed to be returned to the 5th ring of the Nether – that's where they live."

"Yeah, and you know what *else* lives on the 5th ring?

Other Class 5s, like that Netherbat that wanted to snack on my head."

"Tabitha was entirely correct in doing what she did," Pinch said, coming quickly to her defence. "The *Nightmare Division's Guide to the Nether* is quite clear on the matter – rules are, after all, *rules*!"

"Well, you know how much I love rules, Pinch," Rex replied. "Without 'em, I'd have nothing to break."

"I've had enough of this," Mr Benjamin said. "Can any of you give me one good reason why I shouldn't call the police?"

"I'll give you one," Tabitha replied, turning to him. "Your son, Charlie, is as strong with the Gift as I've ever seen. But if he doesn't learn to control it... *he'll kill you all*."

CHAPTER THREE

THE SMELL OF CINNAMON

"THEY CLAIM TO know what's been going on with Charlie," Barrington said to Olga in the living room several minutes later, after everyone had cleaned up. "I think we should listen to them."

"So do I," Charlie agreed, sitting on the couch next to her.

Olga just shrugged.

"Look, I know this isn't the first time something like this has happened around here," Tabitha said, perched on the floral-print armchair next to the couch. "You've been looking for answers. We can give them to you."

"Absolutely," Rex agreed, cracking his knuckles. Tabitha winced. "Here's the thing: all kids dream, right? Sometimes you get good dreams and sometimes you get nightmares. But nightmares aren't just in your head – they have a purpose. They're like a doorway that opens into boogey-boogey land."

"The correct term is the *Netherworld*," Pinch corrected.

"And in this *boogey-boogey land*," Rex continued, glaring at him, "are tons of nasty little critters that want to come through that doorway and into our world."

"Why?" Charlie asked.

"They like to cause problems," Rex said. "Most of 'em are just a nuisance. They bang around in old houses, scare old ladies, that kinda thing."

"Ghosts!" Charlie said.

"Yeah, that's one type. You don't have to worry about them too much – they're basically harmless. But some of 'em, Charlie... some of 'em are *deadly*. Like those Class 5s we just spanked."

"So, you're saying these 'things' come into our world all the time?" Mr Benjamin asked in disbelief.

"That's right," Tabitha answered. "But they need kids to do it. Kids with what we call 'the Gift'."

"You're either born with it or you're not," Rex said with a shrug.

"The Gift is fuelled by imagination," Tabitha continued, "which, by adulthood, has usually become a sad and crippled thing. The stronger the Gift, the larger and more powerful the portal that can be created and the more dangerous the creature that can come through." She smiled reassuringly at Charlie. "Your son... he's unusually strong."

"Absolutely," Pinch agreed. "It's been decades since a child was powerful enough to portal in a Class 5. I've had my eye on him for some time actually – ever since the Naptime Catastrophe."

"You *heard* about that?" Charlie gasped.

"Of course I did. I wouldn't be good at my job if I didn't keep tabs on such things, now would I? But it wasn't until the recent newspaper article that I knew we had to act quickly."

"Newspaper article? You mean, 'Terror at the Sleepover Apocalypse'?" Barrington asked.

Pinch nodded. "It was clear from the story that your son had portalled through a fairly sizeable Netherstalker – at least a Class 3."

"What's a Netherstalker?" Charlie asked.

"It looks something like a giant spider," Tabitha replied.

"See!" Charlie yelled triumphantly, turning to his parents. "Told you."

"I knew immediately that we needed to get to your boy," Pinch continued, "to prevent him from being a danger to himself or others. As you can see from the events of this evening, it's lucky that we did."

Barrington shook his head in amazement. "So all this time we thought Charlie was going on a rampage during his nightmares, he was actually allowing monsters into our world and *they* were the ones causing the destruction?"

"That's right," Pinch replied.

"Utterly amazing," Barrington said, and turned to Olga. "Don't you agree, dear?"

She shrugged, seemingly uninterested.

Rex stared at her curiously. "I notice you haven't said a word, Mrs Benjamin. You mind if I ask, were you baking cinnamon buns today?"

"No," she said.

"Cinnamon cookies, cinnamon rolls, cinnamon toast? Anything with cinnamon in it?"

"Not that I recall," she said.

"Did you eat anything with cinnamon? Or maybe one of your friends did?"

"I don't think so."

"I thought not," Rex continued, then suddenly leaped across the coffee table and grabbed her by the throat. *"What have you done with Charlie's mum, you disgusting thing?"*

Mr Benjamin stared in shock as Rex throttled his wife.

"What on Earth..." he gasped. "Inappropriate! Inappropriate!"

"Let go of my mother!" Charlie shouted, leaping across the coffee table. He grabbed Rex and tried to pull his hands from his mother's throat.

"This ain't your mother, kid," Rex said. "You smell that? Cinnamon. All Mimics reek of it."

"Let her go this instant," Pinch demanded. "Many people smell of cinnamon who are *not* creatures from the Netherworld!"

"Maybe so, but this one is and I'll prove it to you," Rex said, and dragged Mrs Benjamin from the couch as her husband squealed in disapproval.

"That is my wife you are dragging by the neck, sir! I will not stand for this! Stop immediately!"

But Rex ignored him as he carried Mrs Benjamin towards the downstairs bathroom. She bit and clawed wildly at his face, particularly when he flung open the shower door and roughly threw her in.

"What are you doing?" Charlie yelled.

"You'll see."

"Don't let him hurt Mummy!" Olga pleaded. "Help Mummy. Mummy always protected *you*!"

"Knock it off, Mimic," Rex snapped, and turned on the shower.

As soon as the water hit Olga, she shrieked with an inhuman wail and scrabbled frantically at the glass of the shower door. Her skin began to bubble and blacken; then it peeled off in large strips, liquefying before running down the drain. When it was all over, the thing that had been impersonating Mrs Benjamin writhed sluglike around the shower floor. It was pink and doughy, with two large eyes, no legs and two extremely long and powerful arms.

Mr Benjamin and Charlie stared in shock.

"Feast your eyes on a Class-4 Mimic," Rex said with a slight "I told you so" swagger. "You can tell it's a 4 by the number of fingers on each hand. The more fingers it has, the more powerful it is."

"Quite right," Pinch chimed in. "A Class 1, for instance, is only strong enough to subdue and mimic something the size of an infant, but it would take a full-fledged Class 5 to turn a grown man like you into its prey."

"Its *prey*..." Mr Benjamin said with growing anxiety.

"Yes, but don't worry," Tabitha said, placing a calming hand on his shoulder. "For a Mimic to maintain a disguise, its victim has to be close by and *alive*. Your wife is fine. It probably snatched her out of bed when it came through during one of Charlie's latest nightmares and hid her somewhere in the house before taking her shape."

"The attic," Charlie said. "I heard scratching around up there last night. I thought it was squirrels."

Tabitha turned to Rex. "You go get her. I'll get rid of this." She gestured to the Mimic, which struggled in vain to reach above the shower doors with its long, powerful fingers.

"No offence, sweetheart," Rex replied, "but you're just a Portal Jockey. Why don't I stay and give you a hand?"

"The day I need help disposing of a common Mimic is the day I say I love you."

"Meaning?"

"Never," she said, and waved him goodbye.

The attic was dark and smelled like old newspapers and wet mattresses. Mr Benjamin climbed the ladder first, followed by Charlie.

"Mum?" Charlie shouted.

"My dear? Are you up here?"

As they searched, Pinch pulled Rex aside. "You will never again pull a stunt like that. What if you had been wrong about the Mimic?"

"I wasn't," Rex replied.

"But if you had been and you ended up hurting that woman, the ND could have been compromised."

"It wasn't."

Pinch rolled his eyes. "Decisions that affect the operational integrity of the Nightmare Division are solely my domain. *I* interpret the rules. *I* make the call. *You* carry it out. Simple as that."

"No, it's not that simple," Rex said, leaning in. "My gut told me something was wrong with that woman and I gotta trust it. You wouldn't understand what that's like. You don't have the Gift. At least not any more."

Pinch recoiled as if stung.

"Sorry, Pinch," Rex continued. "I didn't mean it like that. It's just that I gotta act on what I think is right."

"So do I," Pinch said. "And if you ever again make a decision without my approval, I will recommend to the Council that you be placed on probation."

"I'm sure you will."

"Hey, everyone! Get over here!" Charlie yelled. "We found her – she's in the spaceship!"

Olga Benjamin had spent the last two days stuffed into an old, forgotten refrigerator box that Charlie and his father had painted to look like a spaceship. Her hands and feet were bound with masking tape and her mouth was gagged with a dirty dust rag.

"My poor dear..." Mr Benjamin said as he tore off the masking tape and removed the gag from her mouth.

"Are you all right?"

"I thought I was dead," Olga said, her voice raspy from disuse. "There was a creature... a hideous thing with long, terrible fingers... It *abducted* me... It put me in the spaceship..."

"We know all about it, Mum," Charlie said. "It was disgusting! But it's gone now – Rex and Tabitha got rid of it."

"Rex and who?" Olga croaked.

"There's a great deal of information you need to be made aware of," Mr Benjamin replied, helping her to her feet. "Let's get you a cup of tea to calm your nerves."

The tea (and the whisky mixed into it) did help calm Olga's nerves. As she sipped her third cup, she listened carefully as Rex spun a story of Portal Jockeys (*"Nethermancers,"* Tabitha gently corrected him), Banishers, Class-5 Silvertongues in full voice, the smell of cinnamon and how water exposes a Mimic.

"But why on Earth would it *want* to mimic me?" Olga asked.

"Sweat, ma'am," Rex said. "Your garden-variety Mimic loves sweat. In fact, they need it to survive. They'll take it from animals if they can't get it from humans, but in order to lap it up, they have to disguise themselves as something with a mouth – they don't have one of their own, you see."

"Er, exactly *whose* sweat was the Mimic drinking?" Mr Benjamin asked with some alarm.

"Yours probably," Rex said with a grin. "While you were sleeping, most likely. There's nothing a Mimic likes more than to lick the sweat off a fella while he's catching forty winks."

"I see," Mr Benjamin said, blood draining from his face.

"So, what do we do now?" Olga asked.

"Now," Pinch replied, eyes bright with excitement, "we need to take the boy for a hearing at the High Council of the Nightmare Division."

"The what?" Mr Benjamin asked.

"I'm glad you don't know!" Pinch snapped. "You see, the Nightmare Division is an incredibly *secret* organisation, charged with controlling the Nethercreature population. As you can imagine, with all the nightmares in the world, there is a vast array of Nethercreatures that must be accounted for and disposed of."

"Yes, yes, but what do they want with *Charlie*?" Mr Benjamin pressed.

Pinch seemed aghast that the answer wasn't completely obvious. "Anyone with the unusual strength to portal a Class 4 or greater Nethercreature must be brought before the Council to be identified, processed and evaluated. It is quite mandatory. The rules are very specific."

"Is this true?" Olga asked, turning to Tabitha.

"I'm afraid it is," she answered. "But don't worry. I would do anything it took to protect Charlie."

"And what exactly would he need to be protected *from*?" Olga pressed. "What might they choose to do with him, I mean?"

"Oh, that just depends," Pinch said with obvious relish. "They may decide the boy is trainable and place him in the Nightmare Academy. In a few years, he will graduate and, like us, spend his life ridding the world of Nethercreatures. Very honourable."

"Yeah, a dream come true," Rex said wryly.

"And if they decide he is *not* trainable?" Mr Benjamin prompted.

"Well, you can't very well let a child with the ability to portal a Class 5 just run around bringing monsters into our world hither and thither," Pinch replied. "I mean, can you imagine what would have happened if we had not been there to banish the Silvertongue? Can you even fathom what would occur if he was strong enough to portal in a *Named*?" Pinch said the word *Named* with an involuntary shudder, and Charlie wondered what kind of creature could be so horrible that it frightened Pinch even more than the terrifying monsters they had already faced.

"No," Pinch continued with a nervous laugh, "if the Council decided he was not trainable, then Charlie would need to be... Reduced."

"'Reduced'?" Olga asked.

"Yes. Reduction is a process by which our top surgeons, quite painlessly and through the most cutting edge of techniques, *reduce* the amount of creative thought the boy is capable of, thereby *reducing* his ability to portal anything above, say, a Class 2."

"I see," said Mr Benjamin. "You will surgically make the boy stupid."

"Not at all, not stupid, no, sir," Pinch countered. "Your boy has an extraordinary number of IQ points. We would just shave off a few."

"'Shave off a few'?" Mr Benjamin repeated.

"Absolutely. He's got so many, he would hardly miss them."

"I see," said Mr Benjamin, turning to his wife. "Thoughts?"

"I think if they try to take Charlie," she said sweetly, "I will personally rip off their heads and plant flowers in their throats."

"Well put," Mr Benjamin replied.

Charlie leaped up. "Don't I have a say in any of this? It's about me, after all."

"Son, you can't possibly want to go with these people," Mr Benjamin protested. "In the best of worlds, you will be taken from us and turned into some kind of monster hunter and, in the worst, you will be made stupid."

"Just average," Pinch countered.

"Even worse!" Mr Benjamin snapped. "You cannot have him."

"But I *want* to go," Charlie said. "This is the first time I've ever understood why these things were happening to me. I want to learn more. I want to do what they do."

"Out of the question," Mr Benjamin said.

"I'm sorry, Charlie, but our no is final," Olga seconded.

"It's beyond that now," Pinch said, standing. "The rules are quite clear. We are to bring him before the Council with or without your consent – by force, if necessary."

Mr Benjamin leaped to his feet. "It will have to be by force then. If you think you're stronger than my love for my son, I invite you to take your best shot, sir." He rolled up his sleeves and flexed his scrawny arms.

Mrs Benjamin turned to Tabitha and Rex. "You're good people," she pleaded. "*Do something*."

"Much as I hate to say it, ma'am," Rex said, "Pinch is right. Because of Charlie, you spent the last few days tied up in a cardboard box – and that's just from a stupid Mimic. If another Class 5 comes through or, worse, a Named... it's all over – for you and your husband and for Charlie too. If you want to protect him, you gotta let him come with us. Only once before have I seen someone this strong with the Gift."

"What happened to that one?" Olga asked.

"That one went bad," Rex said quietly. "This one won't. You have my word. That may not mean much from other folks, but it means a lot from me."

Olga seemed unconvinced. "Barrington... what should we do?"

Mr Benjamin considered, then turned to Rex. "If you hurt my son," he said, "if anything happens to him – even so much as a knuckle scrape – there will be no place in this wide world for you to hide from my wrath. Am I understood?"

"You are," Rex said.

Charlie was shocked – he had never seen his father so forceful before. He felt a surprising blush of pride.

Barrington took Olga's hand in his. "My dear, I know it's hard to imagine letting him go... but I think it's for the best. Perhaps it's time to let his destiny reveal itself."

"But he's so *little*," she protested.

"I'll be fine, Mum," Charlie said. "Trust me."

"I *do* trust you, Charlie," she replied. "It's them I'm not so sure about…" She gestured to Rex, Tabitha and Pinch.

"I understand how you feel, ma'am," Rex said. "I know we squabble and argue and maybe don't look like the most trustworthy folks in the world. If I were in your shoes, I'd feel the same way. But I promise you, we won't let anything happen to your boy." Rex smiled gently. "See, ma'am, I grew up on a ranch, and my daddy always said, 'If the milk is sour, move the herd' – well, things have been sour here for a while and gettin' worse. If you love him… if you want to *save* him… you gotta let him go."

Olga searched his eyes to see if he was telling the truth.

"Take him then," she said finally and began to cry.

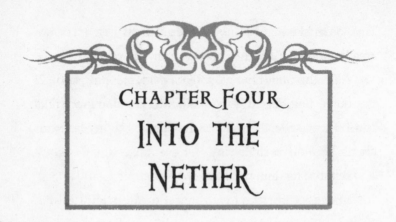

CHAPTER FOUR
INTO THE NETHER

T HE NIGHT-TIME air felt good on Charlie's face. He and the three adults strode quickly from his house. "She thinks I'm a baby," Charlie said, adjusting the overnight bag slung over his shoulder. He had quickly packed a couple of pairs of jeans, a few favourite shirts and his Gadget Journal.

"She's just concerned about you," Tabitha replied, ruffling his hair. "You're her only child."

"But she thinks I can't do *anything*. I'm brave. I'm tough. I can do stuff."

"Little mouths have big appetites," Rex said with a grin.

"What's that supposed to mean?"

"It means be careful what you wish for. You'll have adventure soon enough – more than you want probably.

This looks like a good spot." Rex gestured to a shadowy area behind a large bush, hidden from the street.

"All right. Stand back," Tabitha said, stepping behind the bush. She closed her eyes and extended her right hand. Purple flames began to crackle across her body as the air became electric.

"What's she doing?" Charlie asked.

"Making a portal so we can get to the High Council pronto," Rex explained. "We could have done it back at the house, but I figured we should scram from there before your folks changed their minds. They seemed like they were wavering when Pinch gave them those envelopes addressed to the 'Nightmare Division'."

"It's the only way they can contact Charlie," Pinch replied. "I thought it would ease their fears."

"Well, *my* fears won't be eased until we get outta here. Don't worry, kid – Portaljumps are usually fast."

"And risky," Pinch added.

"You take all the risk outta life, Pinch. You take out all the fun too."

Suddenly, a two-metre-high portal opened in front of them, its circular rim arcing with purple flame. Through it, Charlie could see a barren, rocky plain. It was a desolate place with large, oddly shaped outcroppings of stone dotted with sickly-looking scrub brush that had a bluish cast to it. It looked very different from the part of the Nether that Charlie had seen earlier.

"Hop on through," Rex said, ushering Charlie towards the open gateway.

Charlie turned to him nervously. "But isn't it full of..."

"Monsters?" Rex said, grinning. "Trust me, it's perfectly safe. Go on."

Charlie took a breath, closed his eyes and stepped into the Netherworld.

After a slight *whooshing* sensation, he found himself standing alone on the hard, stony soil. He looked behind him to see Pinch, Rex and Tabitha step through. With a quick wave of her hand Tabitha closed the portal, and Charlie almost cried out in alarm. He felt a kind of panic: he was stranded in an alien world and, like a scuba diver who had gone too deep and forgotten which way was up, Charlie realised that he had absolutely no idea how to get out.

"Relax, kid," Rex said, seeing his rising panic. "Take a breath. Look around. Get your bearings."

Charlie forced himself to steady his nerves and then did as Rex suggested. He was surprised to discover that the rocks surrounding them all subtly leaned in the same direction, as if pointing. He turned to see what they were pointing *at* and found himself staring at a giant pillar of red fire, twisting and writhing far in the distance.

"That's the Inner Circle," Rex said, stepping up beside him. "Look but don't touch – nasty place."

"How far is it?" Charlie asked, awestruck.

"In kilometres? No idea, but *far*. Real far. Right now, we're on the 1st ring – the outermost ring of the Nether. See, it's helpful to think of the Nether as a kind of bull's-eye, with smaller rings inside bigger ones. It's pretty safe out here on the 1st ring, just your odd Gremlin and Wight roaming around – nothing more serious then a Class-1 critter in any case. But the closer you get to the centre, the more dangerous the things that live there."

"Why?" Charlie asked.

"Because the Inner Circle draws all the monsters of the Nether to it," Pinch answered, jumping in. "They start out here on the 1st ring, frail and weak – baby Silvertongues, Mimics, Netherbats and so forth – but as they mature, they migrate towards the centre. It's simply what they're born to do."

"Yeah," Rex added. "Most of 'em don't make it all the way to the Inner Circle – they get killed along the way. But the ones that do... they're the worst of the worst, kid. It takes them a lotta years to make the trip from here to there, and the journey is so brutal that it makes 'em either get strong or get dead. What do you see past this open plain?"

Charlie looked and saw that the flat, moonlike ground they stood on eventually gave way to a dark forest, thick and impenetrable. "A forest," he said. "At least that's what it looks like from here."

Rex nodded. "We call that the 2nd ring. Anything that can survive in there is, by definition, a Class 2. And if you look just past the forest, what do you see?"

"Mountains," Charlie said. The colour of bleached bones, they rose into the sky like jagged teeth. "Is that the 3rd ring?"

"Yup," Rex replied. "And that's where you'd find the Class-3 versions of those same critters as they move towards the Inner Circle, getting stronger and more vicious every day. See how it works?"

Charlie nodded. "So what's past the mountains? What does the 4th ring look like?"

"It's an ocean," Rex said. "Vast and cold and deep. In fact, I nicknamed it 'The Chill Depths'."

"Chill Depths?" Pinch replied with a scowl. "That's a ridiculous name."

"What do *you* call it then?"

"The 4th ring, of course!"

"But if you *had* to give it a nickname," Rex pressed, "what would it be?"

Pinch thought for a moment. "'the Terrifying Ocean'," he said finally.

"The Terrifying Ocean?" Rex roared. "That's terrible! Where's the beauty? Where's the *poetry*?"

"I have a question," Charlie said. "If it's just an ocean, where do the Class-4 versions of creatures like the Silvertongue live? Do they learn to breathe water?"

"Excellent query," Pinch answered, "and no, they do not. You see, the 'Terrifying Ocean'" – he shot a challenging look at Rex – "is not *all* ocean. There are islands there as well... but not the kind you're used to. Much of it is still uncharted. In fact, only a very small percentage of the Nether has ever been explored."

"That's true," Rex continued. "And past the Chill Depths," – he shot a look at Pinch – "is the 5th ring. You saw a glimpse of it earlier, through the portal in your bedroom."

"Where those yellow crystals were?" Charlie asked.

Rex nodded. "It's a terrible place. I'm sure it was kind of hard to tell, looking down on it from where we were, but at ground level, you'd see it's tight and claustrophobic and filled with the oldest and most deadly critters in the Nether."

"Except for those in the Inner Circle," Pinch corrected.

"Except for those," Rex conceded.

"I can't believe I opened a portal near *that*," Charlie said softly, pointing to the tornado of red flame in the distance.

"Near but not *in*, thank goodness," Pinch said. "You don't ever want to open a portal inside the Inner Circle. That's where the Named live."

Once again, Pinch shuddered at the mention of the word.

"In case you haven't noticed, Pinch is a little panicky when it comes to the Named," Rex said, but before Charlie could question him further, Rex turned to Tabitha. "How about that portal?"

"Just waiting for you to stop lecturing the boy," she said, and extended her right hand. Purple flames began to crawl across her body.

"What's she doing now?" Charlie asked.

"Opening another portal to the Nightmare Division," Rex explained. "See, you can only open portals *into* the Netherworld and *out of* the Netherworld, so if you want to go quickly from place to place on Earth, you gotta portal into the NW, step through, then open another portal leading to the place on Earth where you wanna end up."

"So when you portal into the Nether," Charlie said, "you would probably only want to portal into the 1st ring, where we are right now, because that's the safest place?"

"Kid's got it all figured out already," Rex said with a grin. Just then, Charlie noticed that the short sword and lasso looped on Rex's belt began to glow with a dim blue fire. Rex saw it too and, quick as a flash, he spun and cracked his lasso at a group of small, spindly creatures with large grey eyes and long tails. They instantly ran off in a chorus of frightened screeches, scattering into the rocks like roaches.

"Gremlins," Rex said, casually looping his lasso back on to his belt. "They're the trash of the Nether. They don't even have a class number, because they never grow any bigger. They're basically harmless over here, but on the Earth side they like to chew on electric cables. They can cause real problems – cars malfunctioning, power plants crashing, that kind of thing."

Suddenly, with a *pop*, the new portal Tabitha created opened in front of them. Charlie looked through it and was shocked to see a lion staring back, its mane a full and glorious crown of hair, its teeth as thick as a man's finger and nearly as long. The lion opened its mouth and roared. The sound was deafening and made Charlie's entire body vibrate. He yelped and stumbled backwards.

"Don't worry," Rex said, laughing. "It won't hurt you. Step on through. You'll see."

Charlie, not moving, stared at Rex, unsure.

"Trust me," Rex said with a smile.

Cautiously, Charlie stepped through the portal.

After feeling that familiar *whooshing* sensation, Charlie found himself standing beside a rock wall. The lion padded towards him, and Charlie was shocked to discover just how big it was up close. He would barely make an appetiser for the beast, much less a main course.

The lion drew to within thirty centimetres of him and sniffed deeply. Charlie froze. His heart beat wildly in his chest and he couldn't breathe. Then the lion opened its mouth, leaned forwards... *and licked his face.*

Charlie stumbled back, shocked. "Why is it licking me?" he managed to gasp. From somewhere behind him, he heard Rex laugh.

"What do you smell?"

Charlie closed his eyes and breathed in slowly. "Cinnamon..."

"Which means?"

"The lion's a Mimic, isn't it?" Charlie said, suddenly putting it together.

"That's right," Rex nodded. "It doesn't want to eat you; it just wants your sweat. The real lions are safe and sound in a cage just below us."

"Where are we now?"

"Look for yourself."

Rex gestured for Charlie to walk around the rock wall beside him. Charlie tentatively did so and found himself standing in the midst of three other lions. Surrounding them was a moat of water. Beyond the moat was a fence and past that... people – many of them.

Rex clapped him on the shoulder. "We're in the lion enclosure in the San Diego Zoo. This is one of the entrances to the Nightmare Division."

"But *why*?" Charlie asked.

"Privacy, of course," Pinch said with a hint of impatience. "No one else knows the lions are just Class-5 Mimics. They wouldn't dare approach the door."

"Door?"

"Follow me," Pinch said, and strode confidently towards a cave on the far side of the enclosure.

"Come on, kid," Rex said with a friendly wink. "Keep up."

Charlie followed the three adults through the pride of fake lions and into the cave. At the far end, out of view of the public, stood a large metal door with no hinges or doorknobs. It had a small black plate in the very centre.

"All right, who's gonna open it?" Rex asked.

"Not me," Tabitha answered. "I hate this part."

"I did it last time," Pinch added quickly.

"Great," Rex said with a sigh. He leaned up to the small black plate and stuck out his tongue. Instantly, a pair of metal tongs shot out and clamped down on the tip of it.

"What's it doing?" Charlie asked.

"Tething by D Ben A," mumbled Rex.

"Testing his DNA, he's trying to say," Pinch explained. "The doors of the Nightmare Division are protected by Salivometers. Your saliva contains your entire genetic make-up, and the machine uses that to identify people."

"*Henderson, Rexford – identity confirmed,*" a computer voice chimed soothingly. The tongs released Rex's tongue and slid back to their hiding place behind the black plate.

"God, I hate that," he said, flexing his jaw.

Suddenly, the metal door whispered open and Charlie got his first glimpse into the Nightmare Division.

The place was a technological marvel, a monstrosity of chrome and steel. From what Charlie could see, it was absolutely gigantic, much larger than he'd expected, and it was alive with activity. Computer terminals lined the hallways and Salivometers controlled access to the many identical doors that dotted the walls of the main terminal.

Throngs of workers moved purposefully through the cavernous area. Two men in purple tracksuits wheeled a tank with a large squidlike creature past a woman in a yellow tracksuit pushing a cart with a giant plate of spaghetti and meatballs on it. At least Charlie *thought* they were meatballs, until they blinked. With a shock, he realised that they were actually *eyes*, which meant that the stuff he thought was spaghetti was— But before he could investigate further, the yellow tracksuited woman was gone, arrowing down one of the many hallways that radiated out from the terminal.

"The ND can be a little overwhelming," Rex said, almost as if reading Charlie's mind. "But it's just a job site like any other. Stick with us, don't touch anything and we'll get to the High Council in no time."

They walked quickly through a maze of hallways, passing doors with exotic-sounding descriptions like GNOME JUICING FACILITY (CLASS 3 AND BELOW) and VENOMOUS SERPENT DEFANGING CLINIC (NO KRAKENS!).

Just a job site like any other, Charlie thought, his mind reeling.

Suddenly, a man on a gurney rolled towards them,

pushed by two workers in red tracksuits. The man's entire body had gone a brilliant shade of marble white. It wasn't until he was wheeled past them that Charlie realised the man wasn't just the colour of marble; he was actually *made* of marble. He was as solid and still as a sculpture.

"Poor guy," Tabitha said.

"That's what happens when you look at a Gorgon," Rex muttered, shaking his head. "Guess he won't do that again."

"Can they help him?" Charlie asked.

"Yeah, if they can find the Gorgon that turned him into stone and then cut off her head – easier said than done."

They stopped at a pair of large chrome doors. The sign on them read THE HIGH COUNCIL – ABSOLUTELY NO ADMITTANCE WITHOUT PRIOR AUTHORISATION!

"We're here," Rex said, and led them inside.

CHAPTER FIVE
THE HIGH COUNCIL

CHARLIE HAD NEVER seen anything quite like it before. The High Council chamber was the world's largest and most imposing courtroom. The sleek logo of the Nightmare Division (an intertwined *N* and *D*) took up the entire wall at the far end of the room. Below the logo, on a raised dais, sat twelve Council members in identical dark suits. Presiding over them was a grey-haired man with a prominent nose and steely eyes. A placard identified him: REGINALD DRAKE – DIRECTOR.

"That guy in the centre is the one we'll be talking to," Rex whispered, trying not to interrupt a meeting that was clearly already in progress. "He's the Director of the Nightmare Division."

"He'll decide what happens to me?" Charlie asked.

"He decides what happens to *everyone*."

A young man stood before the Director, making an impassioned plea with a variety of visual aids. He seemed nervous in the presence of the thirteen people who towered above him, all of them staring grimly.

"The Gremlin population has increased twelve per cent in just two years," the young man said, gesturing to a chart that demonstrated his statistic. "Drastic measures are needed. They have infiltrated the California and New York power grids to such an extent that rolling blackouts are all but inevitable this year."

"How did this happen?" Director Drake snapped. "Are you not in charge of keeping the Gremlin population thinned? Is that not your job, sir?"

"It is," the young man admitted, "but we have been unable to Banish them at the same rate they've been coming into the world. As the human population expands" – he gestured to another chart, which read "Human Population Expanding at Dramatic Rate" – "there are a greater number of children who unwittingly portal them in during their nightmares – which are *also* becoming more frequent, due to uneasiness over the current scary state of world events. The power grids can't sustain the constant attack. I mentioned California and New York, but the Gremlins are having a serious impact *globally* as well. Our London Division is reporting significant disruptions throughout Piccadilly Circus, and I haven't even *begun* to address what our colleagues in Spain, Italy and Korea are telling us. We're looking at an epidemic."

"I certainly hope you haven't come before me to whine about your failures," the Director shot back. "Please tell me you have a *plan*."

"Of course we do, Director," the young man quickly assured him. "Are you aware of the great success we've been having with our Mimic Motels?"

"You're talking about those ugly, fake motels you've been building around the country?"

"Yes, Director. Every room has an open vat of sweat, which attracts Mimics by the truckload. Once there, a handful of Nethermancers and Banishers are able to easily return them to the Nether."

"Yes, I know all that," Drake snapped. "Get on with it!"

The young man swallowed hard and continued. "Well, Director, we're proposing to do the same thing with the Gremlins. Because they feed on electricity, we can lure them to a fake power plant under ND control and Banish them as they arrive. It's far more efficient than chasing them around the world, trying to sneak our Banishers into private power plants to deal with the problem piecemeal."

"Sounds dicey," Drake replied, "but I'll approve it,

provided you understand that I am holding you solely responsible. I will expect an update in two months. If the problem is not improving by then, I will also expect your resignation."

"Understood, Director," the young man said. "I won't disappoint you." He hustled towards the door, passing Charlie on his way out. "Good luck," he muttered. "The Director's in a terrible mood."

"Maybe we should come back another time," Charlie whispered to Rex. But before Rex could answer, the voice of the Director roared through the chamber.

"And who is this?" he asked, staring pointedly at Charlie.

Pinch stepped forwards. "Edward Pinch, at your service, Director. We've acquired the boy. The one we've had our eye on."

"Have you?" Drake said. "Excellent. Come here, boy. What's your name?"

"Go on up," Rex whispered. "We're right behind you."

Heart fluttering nervously, Charlie headed down the long centre aisle that led to the High Council. "My name is Charlie, sir. Charlie Benjamin."

"Ah, yes, I remember now. And you may address me as 'Director'. 'Sir' is what you'd call a *waiter*, and I'd like to think I've achieved more than a measly waiter, don't you agree?"

"Yes, sir," Charlie said, nodding. "I mean, yes, *Director*," he quickly added.

Drake gave Charlie a slight grunt, then turned to Pinch. "You confirmed he's strong with the Gift?"

"Indeed, Director. We witnessed him portal a Class-5 Silvertongue."

"A 5, huh?" Drake replied with a whistle. "That's rather extraordinary. Have any other portallings been attributed to him?"

"Well, a day or so earlier, he brought through a Class-4 Mimic that took the place of his mother, and we strongly believe that he was responsible for portalling in a Class-3 Netherstalker that cocooned several children at a sleepover less than a week ago."

"Do you mean to say that, within a *week*, he went from portalling a Class 3 to a Class 5?" Drake asked.

"Exactly," Pinch replied. "Incredible, isn't it? His power is growing remarkably fast. And not only that. Newspaper accounts show that when he portalled the Netherstalker, it cocooned only the other children and left him *completely alone*."

"Unbelievable," Drake remarked.

"Actually, I wondered about that," Charlie said. "Why *did* it leave me alone?"

"Because," Pinch replied, "unlike the more stupid

creatures of the Nether – Gremlins and Ectobogs, for instance – Netherstalkers are quite smart and, unless forced to, will usually refuse to attack a much stronger foe, which you clearly were."

"Wow," Charlie said.

"Wow indeed," Pinch replied. "And perhaps now you will do the Director the courtesy of speaking only when spoken to."

"Oh. Sorry, Director," Charlie said.

Drake shot another grunt in his direction, then turned to Rex and Tabitha. "And what do you two have to say?"

"Well, the child is definitely strong with the Gift," Tabitha replied. "Maybe the strongest I've ever seen."

"Strength is nothing without the ability to *control* it," Drake said.

"Oh, he's trainable," Rex replied. "Absolutely."

"And you base this on..."

"My gut," Rex said. "I can just tell."

"Ah, I see. Well, while you may be comfortable making critical decisions based on your *gut*, I hope you won't mind if I don't place quite the same *faith* in it."

"With all respect, Director, you'll see I'm right after he's spent a year in the Nightmare Academy."

"Oh, he's not going to the Academy," Drake said casually.

"What?" Rex replied, shocked.

"The boy can already portal a Class 5 with no schooling at all! Can you even *imagine* what he'll be capable of if he's allowed to achieve his full power? Opening a portal into the Inner Circle may not be beyond him. The last time that happened, a Named came through, and we have been scrambling to recover from Verminion's escape ever since."

"But the boy may be the *solution* to that problem," Rex pressed. "A kid this powerful, properly trained, could have the ability to return Verminion to the Nether – or kill him outright. Charlie could be our ultimate weapon against the Nethercreatures."

"And he could just as easily be their ultimate weapon against *us*," Drake snapped. "Or have you already forgotten how Verminion got to Earth in the first place?"

"That's fear talking," Rex said. "If we're going to make all our decisions based on *fear*, we may as well just hang it up now."

"And why *shouldn't* we make decisions based on fear?" Drake shot back. "Our very existence is based on fear. If people were not afraid, they would not have nightmares, and if they didn't have nightmares, there would be no portals into the Netherworld. Fear is *fundamental* to what we do here. It is the very foundation of this division!" He shook his head. "Training the boy is too much of a risk. He must be Reduced."

"No!" Charlie gasped.

"Don't worry, kid," Rex said, then turned back to the Director. "You know, Arthur Goodnight would have never let a kid like Charlie get Reduced."

"I'm sure that's true," Drake replied. "And that is why the Council chose me as the *new* Director after his death. Goodnight was always too soft on people with the Gift because he possessed it himself – and that's what killed him."

"It was an accident and you know it."

"Of course it was," Drake agreed smoothly. "But all his training and all his power *still* didn't prevent him from having a nightmare and unwittingly portalling through a Class-5 Acidspitter. He was dead before he even woke up, not to mention the Banishers and Nethermancers who were sent to their graves trying to save him." Drake leaned forward. "As strong as Goodnight was, the Gift still made him a *very real threat.* I don't have the Gift, so I don't have that problem."

"The Gift isn't a *problem,*" Rex countered; "it's a solution. You may not have it, but nearly everyone else here uses it to do the work this division was designed for."

"You misunderstand," Drake said. "I have nothing but the utmost respect for my Gifted employees, but people with the Gift are like 'good dogs' – useful and often kind – but every 'good dog' can have a bad day. The stronger they are, the more damage they do when they bite. And a boy like this one" – he gestured to Charlie – "a bite from him could be *lethal*. Goodnight never understood that... until it killed him. I *do* understand it – and I will act accordingly."

"Look, I'm just asking you to give the boy a *chance*, Director," Rex said. "Charlie is trainable. He can control it. Give him a year at the Nightmare Academy. Let him prove it to you."

"Why wait?" Drake replied. "Let him prove it to me *now*. Let him open a portal right now, *this instant*, to demonstrate his ability to use the Gift on command. Perhaps, if he can prove to me that he has unusual control over his abilities, I might reconsider my judgement."

There was silence in the room. Finally, Tabitha spoke up.

"Director," she said. "It takes weeks to train even the strongest child to open a portal while awake."

"Ah, I see," Drake said. "Isn't that *fear* talking? Fear of failure? Your partner doesn't believe in that. Just ask him."

"The kid'll do it," Rex said.

"What?" Tabitha snapped, turning to him. "No, he won't."

Rex pulled Tabitha aside and whispered harshly to her. "This is Charlie's only shot. You know what'll happened if he blows it."

"But it's never been done before," she countered. "And the *pressure*. Even someone skilled in portalling would struggle to do it under these absurd conditions. Look at him. He's terrified."

"So what?" Rex pressed. "*Use his fear.* If you can get him scared enough, you'll send him into a waking nightmare. That should open a portal."

"But he would have no *control* over it," Tabitha protested. "Even if he could manage it, who knows what it might open into? What if another Class 5 comes through? What if *several* come through?"

"Then we'll deal with it," Rex replied. "You just help him to get that portal open."

"I'm waiting," Director Drake said from his high seat. "You have three minutes before I issue my final decision on the boy's fate."

"Go," Rex said to Tabitha. "Make it happen."

"Close your eyes," Tabitha whispered to Charlie moments later, "and listen to me very carefully."

"OK," Charlie said, shutting his eyes.

"Good." Her voice was calm and measured. Soothing. Hypnotic. "You're standing on top of a tall building, Charlie – the tallest you've ever seen."

A picture instantly formed in Charlie's imagination. He saw himself standing on the roof of a building so high that it rose above the clouds. It seemed so real and vivid that he could actually feel the chill breeze stinging his face as the building swayed sickeningly beneath him, buffeted by the wind.

"Do you see it?" she asked. Charlie nodded. "Now... look over the edge."

In his mind's eye, Charlie stepped forwards and peered over the edge of the building. The view was dizzying, hundreds of floors straight down. His stomach lurched nauseatingly and he tasted hot copper in his mouth. He desperately wanted to retreat.

"Suddenly, you feel a hand on your back," Tabitha continued, and Charlie straightened up stiffly. He could actually *feel* the hand. "It pushes you over the side."

"What?" Charlie demanded.

"There's nothing you can do to stop it. You fall."

And, just like that, in his imagination, Charlie fell.

The windows of the skyscraper rushed past him at blinding speed as he plummeted towards the ground far below. He tried to scream, but the air froze his lungs and his heart thudded in his chest like a jackhammer.

"As the ground races towards you," Tabitha continued with more intensity now, "you look towards the windows of the building and see people you know. Your mother and father are in one of them and they could reach out and pull you to safety if they wanted to... but they let you fall."

"Why?" Charlie said, his voice cracking.

"Because life is easier for them without you."

"No..."

"In other windows, you see kids from your past," she continued. "They could all rescue you if they wanted to... but they don't."

"Why not?"

"Because you're not like them, Charlie, and they fear and despise you for it. So they let you fall."

"No one will help me?" he asked.

"No one," Tabitha said. "You're all alone. The ground is coming towards you quickly now and you know that when you hit it, you will die."

"Make it stop," Charlie said.

"I can't help you either, Charlie. You can only help yourself."

"How?"

"Look for a door. A way out. *Do you see one?*"

"No," he shouted, looking around frantically. There were no doors anywhere, just the blur of the windows and the certainty of the hard pavement spiralling towards him.

Then suddenly – "Yes!" he said. "I see one. It's in the ground below me. It's purple. I'm falling towards it, *right at it*."

"Then open it, Charlie. Open it and fall through."

"I don't know if I can," he shouted.

"Open the door!" Tabitha said fiercely. "Open the door now *or you will die*!"

A heartbeat before Charlie hit the ground, he opened the door.

A shudder like an earthquake rolled through the High Council chamber and, with a deafening *boom*, a gigantic portal opened up in front of Charlie, far larger than any he had seen so far. It was the size of a two-storey building and it sliced through the room above and below them. Purple flames danced on its edges.

"Oh, no," Pinch said, backing away.

"Uh-oh..." Rex said, doing the same.

Looking through the portal, Charlie could see an enormous throne room carved from shiny black obsidian.

It was as big as several football fields, and hundreds of Nethercreatures scuttled through it, carrying on their dark business. There were Silvertongues there, as well as creatures Charlie didn't recognise – Banshees and the shadowy, blind Nameless. One by one, they stopped what they were doing and noticed the giant gateway that had opened up before them.

"Close it," Director Drake gasped. "Close the portal *now*, boy. *This instant.*"

But Charlie couldn't hear him. He was lost in his own head, staring in awe at the wonder he had created. Rex rushed to his side and shook him violently.

"Snap out of it, kid," he said. "This is more than we can handle, trust me."

But Charlie barely noticed him. He felt disconnected from his body, separate somehow. Rex and Tabitha and the High Council chamber seemed to exist in another world, far away, one he could barely see. Suddenly, with a shriek, the Nethercreatures rushed towards the open portal, claws snapping, gaping mouths yawning wide.

"You!" Drake screeched, turning to Tabitha. "Shut down the portal! *Shut it now!*"

Tabitha instantly extended her right hand and closed her eyes as Rex unlooped his lasso from his belt, moving to her side. "Just do your best, sweetheart," he said. "I'll keep 'em off you as long as I can."

Purple flames crackled over Tabitha's body and her brow furrowed in fierce concentration. Sweat beaded on her forehead and her breathing came in quick, harsh gasps. She began to shudder.

"*I can't,*" she said finally, opening her eyes. "The portal's too strong."

"Stand back then," Rex said, pushing her behind him. His lasso glowed a fiery electric blue, which grew in intensity as the hundreds of Nethercreatures neared him.

Suddenly, just as the first of the Nethercreatures – a spiderlike Netherstalker – leaped towards the open doorway, a bone-shattering roar was heard from somewhere deep within the throne room. It was so loud that the entire chamber rattled with its echo long after it had stopped. The Nethercreatures froze in their tracks, then scuttled away from the portal, disappearing into the dark recesses of the palace.

Thudding footsteps, each one like the thunder of a cannon, drew closer, until finally, at the far end of the gigantic throne room, a horned creature three storeys high stepped into view. It was powerfully muscled, with orange eyes that glowed like coals and gigantic arms ending in curved talons. Its skin was cobalt blue, dark and deep as a stormy sea, and it had two massive legs, but instead of feet, it had hooves that sparked flame as they slammed into the obsidian floor.

"Barakkas," Pinch gasped.

"Call all the Nethermancers," Drake said, his face now a ghastly shade of white. "Tell them one of the Named is trying to escape from the Nether..."

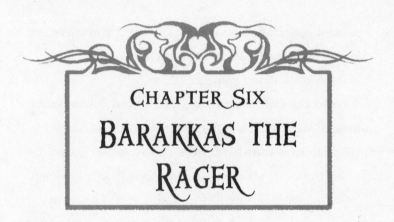

Chapter Six
Barakkas the Rager

Barakkas stepped slowly towards Charlie, flames sparking from his hooves. "Who has come uninvited to my palace?" he growled. "Go ahead, boy. Speak."

"Charlie," Charlie finally managed. "My name is Charlie Benjamin."

"Charlie Benjamin," Barakkas repeated. His voice boomed across the gigantic palace. Even though he was still far away, the echo from the black walls made it seem to Charlie as though the giant creature was standing right next to him. "Only once before has a human breached the Inner Circle."

"I didn't mean to," Charlie said.

"And yet you *did*," Barakkas replied. "You must be very strong."

"I guess so," Charlie said.

"And very *brave*," Barakkas continued, drawing closer. He was now about two football pitches away.

"I never thought I was."

"Who but only the very bravest of boys would dare face me? We have much to talk about, you and I."

As Barakkas talked to Charlie, there was pandemonium in the High Council chamber of the Nightmare Division. Nethermancers poured into the room and quickly found themselves stunned silent when they saw the enormous gateway and the Named creature beyond.

"Stop staring and close the portal, you fools!" Director Drake shrieked.

Recovering from their initial shock, the Nethermancers swung into action and began to try to collapse the portal in on itself. There were fifteen of them in all, both men and women, but their combined efforts seemed to have no more effect on the portal than Tabitha's solo attempt.

"Keep trying!" Drake yelled. "Barakkas is getting closer to the portal!"

Purple firelight arced from Nethermancer to Nethermancer as they vainly struggled to slam shut the doorway. Tabitha joined them, her eyes bright with determination, but soon she realised that even the force of sixteen fully trained adult Nethermancers was no match for the power of the small, slight thirteen-year-old who stood before them in something like a trance.

"What do you want to talk about?" Charlie asked as Barakkas continued his slow, steady walk.

"Your future," Barakkas replied with a smile that revealed many sharp teeth. "I have wonderful things planned for us after I cross through. I need a strong and resourceful apprentice, someone powerful and brave. *Someone like you*. Together, we will wreak havoc upon those who have tormented us."

As Barakkas spoke, Rex sidled up to Charlie and whispered in his ear. "Kid, I know that, deep down, you can hear what I'm saying. You're talkin' to Barakkas the Rager. I know he seems calm and reasonable now, but, trust me, his temper is legendary and you never know what'll set it off. He'll kill you soon as look at you, and when he steps through, death's gonna follow him, you understand? You gotta shut the portal down, son. You're the only one who can do it."

And, somewhere deep in the recesses of Charlie's mind, he *did* hear Rex. It seemed like Rex wanted him to do something, but Charlie wasn't sure what exactly. Something about a bad temper... and a portal...

"Don't listen to him, Charlie," Barakkas said, now only a hundred metres from the open gateway. "He's jealous.

He knows how much more powerful you are than he is, and he *covets* that power. He doesn't want us together because he knows that he will become obsolete. He is a false friend."

"'A false friend...'" Charlie repeated.

"You know that's not true," Rex said. "I told you before I'd protect you no matter what, and now I'm telling you again. You have my word. Shut the portal, kid. *Shut it now.*"

Several of the Nethermancers collapsed from exhaustion; the strain of trying to close what the boy had opened was simply too much.

"Almost there," Barakkas said soothingly, now only several metres from the portal. "Be brave and strong. Hold it open just a moment more."

Barakkas leaned down, preparing to squeeze his gigantic bulk through the gateway. He led with his right arm, his talon claws clenched into a fist. It was the size of a car, that fist. Around his wrist, Charlie could see an enormous metal bracer, glittering blackly. There were intricately carved faces on it – one of which he recognised as the face of Barakkas.

"I just want you to know that none of this is your fault," Rex said as the giant fist pushed out of the portal, dwarfing them. The red patterns that issued from the carved images on the bracer strobed past Charlie's face. "You're a good kid, Charlie. Whatever happens, I just want you to know that."

Just then, Charlie turned. "Rex?" he said, as if seeing him for the first time. "What did you want me to do again?"

"Close the portal, kid," Rex said with a gentle smile.

"OK," Charlie replied and, just like that, the portal slammed shut with a thunderous *crack*, severing Barakkas's right forearm. It thudded to the ground with the force of a wrecking ball, fingers spasming wildly, the enormous bracer throwing dark red light across the chamber in hectic splashes. From somewhere far away, echoing maddeningly across dimensions, Charlie could hear Barakkas scream.

Finally, even that grew silent.

Rex hugged Charlie as the Nethermancers struggled to their feet, glaring at Charlie as if he might, at any moment, attack like a rabid dog. "I didn't mean to do it," he said, seeing the anger and fear on their faces. "It just *happened*."

"It's OK, kid," Rex said, comforting him. "Everything is fine now."

"Everything is most certainly *not* fine," Director Drake

shouted, finding his voice. "It is the very opposite of fine. This child nearly portalled a Named into the very heart of the Nightmare Division. This is exactly what I was afraid of! He could have destroyed us all!"

"You *asked* him to open a portal," Tabitha said as Rex pulled her to her feet. "I told you he wasn't ready."

"Oh, so it's all *my* fault?" Drake sneered. He turned to the Nethermancers. "Take the boy to the Reduction Room immediately. I want him Reduced to the point where he's incapable of portalling so much as a Class-1 Sprite. *I want him made as stupid as a stick!*"

"Rex?" Charlie said with rising panic.

"No worries, kid," Rex said, uncoiling his lasso. With a startling *crack,* it arrowed across the chamber to where it snaked tightly around the Director's neck.

"What are you *doing*?!" Pinch shrieked, horrified.

"I won't let the kid be Reduced. I gave him my word."

"Release me," Drake gasped, his face turning a bright shade of red, "or I will have *you* Reduced as well."

"Good luck with that."

"Let him go," Pinch pleaded. "This will only lead to disaster."

"Better make up your mind quick, Drake," Rex said. "Your face is starting to look like a plum."

Just then, from somewhere at the back of the chamber,

a female voice chimed in. "Up to your old tricks, eh, Rex?"

Charlie turned and saw a tall, regal woman standing there. She had bright blue eyes that shone brilliantly and unexpectedly against the deep, dark chocolate of her skin. Her dress was loose and flowing and was woven from colourful fabrics – buttery yellow, the orange of the sun at dusk mixed with warm, fiery reds. It had a tropical, Jamaican feel that seemed completely out of place in the sterility of the Nightmare Division.

"How's it going, Headmaster?" Rex said.

"Better for me than you, from the looks of it," she replied. "Just can't stay out of trouble, can you?"

"It's a serious failing of mine. I keep hoping I'll outgrow it."

"I won't hold my breath, if you don't mind," she said with a smile. "And, speaking of holding your breath, you'd better let the Director go before he suffocates."

"But—"

"Don't worry about the boy," she interrupted with a wave. "We'll see our way through this."

Rex considered. Then, with a practised flip of the wrist, he uncoiled the lasso from around the Director's neck. Drake greedily gulped air as the bruised colour slowly drained from his face.

The tall woman glanced at the severed arm of

Barakkas, then turned to Charlie. "Looks like someone's done something he shouldn't have," she said with a twinkle in her eye. "I'm Headmaster Brazenhope."

"And I'm—"

"Charlie Benjamin. Yes, I know. I've had my eye on you for some time now."

"Do you know," Drake managed to say, finally catching his breath, "what this little creature has done?"

"Of course I do," the Headmaster replied. "Why else would I be here? To visit you?" She grimaced distastefully. "As soon as I felt the disturbance in the Nether, I portalled over immediately."

"He wants to have the boy Reduced, Headmaster," Tabitha said.

"Oh, of that I have no doubt. He is, after all, a *bureaucrat* – a champion of the status quo, a defender of the average and the mundane. He despises those who possess the Gift because he does not possess it *himself*. This is, unfortunately, an all-too-common attitude among his ilk."

"Spare me your amateur psychology, Headmistress," Drake said.

"Head*master*, if you please," she shot back. "It is a title, just like *Doctor*."

"A little touchy today, aren't we?"

"This coming from the man who can't stand being

94

called 'sir' because it reminds him of his days waiting tables at Red Lobster?"

"*That is enough!*" Drake thundered, blushing slightly. "The boy will be Reduced because he is a grave threat."

"Reliable as ever, Reginald," the Headmaster said. "You never miss an opportunity to destroy what you don't comprehend. I would sooner let you burn the *Mona Lisa* and raze the pyramids of Egypt than let you touch one molecule of this boy's miraculous brain."

"I have made my decision."

"And I have made mine," she replied. "The boy will come with me to the Nightmare Academy. There, he will be trained."

"I forbid it," Drake said, standing and walking towards her. "Don't make this difficult, Brazenhope. I outrank you and you know it." He turned to the assembled Nethermancers. "Take the boy to the Reduction Room immediately."

The Nethermancers looked around warily, not sure how to respond. "Coogan," the Headmaster said, turning to one of them – a tall man with fire-engine red hair. "Would you obey the new Director... or your old Headmaster? The time has come to choose, I'm afraid."

The Nethermancer looked between the irritated, pleading Director and the calm, poised Headmaster. "I'm sorry, Director," he said finally. "I know I report to you... but I owe everything to the Headmaster."

Coogan left the room.

"Susan? Grant? Ryder?" the Headmaster prompted, turning from Nethermancer to Nethermancer. One by one, without a word, they all left. Soon, only Tabitha remained.

"You know where I stand, Headmaster," she said.

The Headmaster turned to Drake. "It seems you're a general without an army, Reginald. Of course, this is the price you pay when you try to inspire fear in your followers instead of respect. Director Goodnight understood that."

"Goodnight is dead."

"That's right," the Headmaster said. "And so, one day, will you be. Nothing is permanent, Reginald – including your reign as Director. Eventually, you will be gone and this division will be restored to its former glory. I plan to be here to see it happen." She fixed him with a withering stare. "The boy will come with me."

Director Drake was furious. Two veins pulsed angrily in his forehead. "Take him," he said finally, "but you alone will be responsible for the consequences."

"I have never sought to place blame elsewhere."

"You may come to regret that," Drake said. "Though

you may have a dubious claim to authority over a child of school age, fully trained Nethermancers and Banishers are clearly under *my* command. So, as of this moment, these two" – he gestured to Rex and Tabitha – "are removed from active duty."

"What?" Tabitha said.

"That's not fair," Rex insisted. "None of this was our fault. Headmaster?"

"Don't look to me for help," she said. "I agree with the Director."

"You can't be serious!" Rex replied in dismay.

"Oh, I'm extremely serious. If you were not removed from active duty, how else would you be available to come to the Academy and *teach*?"

"Teach?" Rex cried out. "I'm a field operator. I don't teach."

"You do now," the Headmaster said. "Both of you. You too, Pinch."

"Me?" Pinch moaned. "What did I do?"

"Nothing," the Headmaster snapped. "And that's your problem." With a casual wave of her hand, she opened a portal. Charlie was shocked to see how easily and quickly she did it – it was a sharp contrast to the time and effort Tabitha required. "Let's go," she said. "The Nightmare Academy awaits."

Seconds later, after a brief stopover in the Nether, the odd group of five stepped through another portal and into a small cabin inside the Nightmare Academy. The walls and floor were built with ancient polished teak boards that gleamed dully in the light of the oil lamp that rested on a large, weathered trunk. Next to the lamp was a glass of warm milk, within reaching distance of the hammock that was strung from wall to wall. The hammock was sewn from an old colourful fabric – mostly reds and ambers – and swayed gently in the tropical breeze that came through a small round window. A hint of moonlight sneaked through as well.

"This is your room, Mr Benjamin," the Headmaster said to Charlie. "You will sleep here tonight. Tomorrow, we will begin your training. The rest of you will come with me. We have much to discuss."

She opened a door and ushered the three adults out.

"Headmaster?" Charlie said. "Will I..."

"Have a nightmare tonight?"

"Yes..."

She smiled warmly. "No. You've had a long day. Tonight is reserved for pleasant dreams and sweet sleep. Drink some milk and go to bed, Mr Benjamin."

Then she left.

Charlie looked through the small round window to try to get a sense of where the Nightmare Academy actually *was*, but the blackness outside was penetrated only by a startling spray of stars that glimmered brilliantly in the night-time sky like cut glass. Within moments, the exhaustion of the day descended upon Charlie like a heavy blanket. He took a gulp of milk, crawled into that soft, welcoming hammock, and felt something he had never truly felt before.

He felt like he *belonged*.

Soon, Charlie fell fast asleep as the warm tropical breeze gently rocked him. From somewhere, he could hear the sound of waves.

Elsewhere in the Nightmare Academy, the adults sat in the Headmaster's study. It was smoky and dim, with flights of stairs and catwalks that led to numerous hazy platforms and landings above. It looked for all the world like the inside of a ship and it was as cluttered and messy as the Nightmare Division had been spare and orderly.

"The boy has made a powerful enemy," the Headmaster said, sipping from a crystal glass filled with a red liquid so dark, it appeared almost black. "Barakkas will not soon forget the one who cost him his hand."

"Serves him right," Rex muttered.

"True," the Headmaster agreed. "But he will hunt the boy to extract his revenge."

"He can't cross over though," Tabitha insisted. "Only you and Charlie are strong enough to open a portal into the Inner Circle, and you certainly won't do it."

"I won't," the Headmaster replied, "but the boy... he's *unpredictable*."

"You can say that again," Pinch muttered.

"You've something to add, Pinch?" the Headmaster said, turning to him. "Speak up."

Pinch mustered his courage. "It was a mistake. The child should have been Reduced. For all our sakes."

"I'm surprised that you, of all people, would advocate that."

"I'm simply being *practical*. You saw what he's capable of! By not Reducing him, we've placed everyone in danger. For all we know, he could be opening another portal to Barakkas's palace even as we speak."

"Not likely," the Headmaster said. "His milk was mixed with an elixir of Dreamless Sleep. There will be no nightmares tonight."

"You actually wasted *elixir* on him?" Pinch asked incredulously. "It would have been cheaper to let the boy drink gold!"

"After all he's been through, he deserves at least *one night* of peace," she replied. Pinch snorted and turned away, dissatisfied. "With proper training," the Headmaster continued, "I believe he can learn to control his portalling. With some precaution and some luck, we will keep Barakkas on his side of the Nether, away from young Mr Benjamin – but Barakkas is not the only threat. There is another, *closer* one."

"You talkin' about Verminion?" Rex asked.

The Headmaster nodded. "When that filthy Named crossed over to Earth, he promptly vanished from sight. We know that for the past twenty years he has been assembling an army of Nethercreatures, drawing them to him as they portal through, but we don't know *where*. It is possible that he could send assassins after the boy... or that he himself could come."

"That's only if he knows about Charlie," Rex said.

"Oh, he knows. He and all the Named would have felt a breach so deep into the Inner Circle. Even I felt it."

"Yeah, but that doesn't mean Verminion is gonna go after the kid who maimed Barakkas," Rex insisted. "The only thing these big boys care about is themselves."

"It is true that Barakkas and Verminion are both Named and, as such, have no particular love for each other," the Headmaster agreed. "But Verminion would know that anyone with the power to so seriously hurt Barakkas could turn that power against him as well. The simple truth is this: Barakkas can't yet get to Charlie, but Verminion *can,* and he will use everything at his disposal to destroy the child."

The Headmaster took another sip from her goblet, which had become dewy with condensation. "There is, however, a silver lining," she said finally. "To come for the boy, Verminion will have to expose himself. It may be the opportunity we've been looking for."

"You mean to use Charlie as bait?" Rex said, rising angrily.

"No," she countered. "I don't mean to *use* him as bait. I mean he *is* bait, whether we like it or not. We must use it to our advantage."

She gestured for Rex to sit. With some reluctance, he did.

"Well, all of this assumes that Verminion knows what Charlie did to Barakkas," Tabitha said. "That he knows how strong Charlie is, how much of a *threat* he could be. The only way he would know that is if the Named have a way of communicating with one another. Do you think they do?"

"I think they *did,*" the Headmaster said grimly.

The chamber of the High Council glowed redly in the light of the bracer that still encircled the wrist of the severed arm of Barakkas. Various workers in blue jumpsuits prepared to lift it on to a waiting gurney to spirit it off to a lab where it could be properly examined and catalogued.

"On three," the crew chief said. He was a large man, who had never met a pie he didn't like. "One, two..." They all lifted at the same time, grunting with effort. After some struggle, they managed to move the arm two metres on to the gurney. "Man," the crew chief said, wiping beads of sweat from his brow. "That's *heavy*."

"It's that thing on its wrist," one of the workers remarked. "There's a tonne of metal there. I wonder what kind."

He reached out to touch it.

Instantly, a red flash like a lightning bolt ripped from the bracer, engulfing him. The light was so intense that it momentarily blinded everyone in the room. When the bright spots finally cleared from their vision, they could see that the worker had been reduced to a pile of ash on the floor.

"Run," the crew chief said as he took off.

The other workers followed, panicked, their herky-jerky shadows spasming across the chamber walls, illuminated by the dark red light of the bracer, which strobed and throbbed, glowing more brightly now than ever before. Unseen by anyone, the carven image of Barakkas seemed to change slightly.

It seemed to smile.

PART TWO

THE NIGHTMARE ACADEMY

Chapter Seven
The Boats in
the Branches

C harlie awoke to find himself staring into the face of a large woman with a wide, round head and round, pink cheeks. In fact, everything about the woman was round. Her hair was pulled into a round, grey bun. Her stomach pressed roundly against the lacy dress she wore. Even her elbows and knees were round.

"Welcome to the world, sleepyhead," she said in a heavy southern American accent.

"What?" Charlie replied, looking around dazedly, not yet fully awake.

"I'm Housemama Rose," she said with a smile. "Now don't get to thinking I'm gonna be here every morning to tend to your every need, but, seeing as how this is your first day, I thought I might as well ease your way into our little corner of the world just this once. Did ya bring clothes?"

"A few things," Charlie replied, gesturing to his overnight bag. As the fog of sleep cleared from his head, he realised that something was wrong. He wasn't sure *what* exactly, but a warning bell buzzed at the back of his brain. He couldn't quite put his finger on it.

"Well, if you need anything else," she said, "socks, underwear, whatever, I'm sure we can scare it up for you."

"Thanks," Charlie said, and suddenly he knew *exactly* what was wrong.

Cinnamon.

The woman smelled like cinnamon.

That warning buzzer in his head turned into a gong, echoing through his skull.

Oh, no, he thought. *I'm all alone with it. What do I do?*

As the thing that claimed to be Housemama Rose babbled on about orientation in an hour and the precise location of the grub hall, Charlie looked around for something he could use as a weapon. His eyes finally came to rest on a small cast-iron pig being used as a doorstop. It looked heavy.

The thing calling itself Housemama Rose turned its back to Charlie, presumably to attend to something behind it. He seized the opportunity to leap from the hammock and sneak across the room to the pig. He lifted it and was surprised to discover that it was even heavier than it looked. His mind raced frantically as he tried to come up with a plan.

He could clout the creature over the head and then make his escape. But what if he missed? Or what if it was stronger than he was? Or he could run and try to find someone to help him before the Housemama Rose thing caught up to him. But what if the hallway outside led only to a locked door?

"Here we go," the creature said, turning back to him. The time for debate was over. He had to act – fast. Charlie raised the cast-iron pig above his head, preparing to strike.

"Oh, my word!" the Housemama Rose thing yelled, stumbling backwards. The silver tray in its hand dropped from its grasp, clattering loudly on the floor, sending the stack of toast and pot of jam on top of it flying.

As Charlie brought the heavy iron pig whistling down towards the thing's head, some small detail registered in his overworked brain.

It was not just toast scattered across the floor.

It was *cinnamon* toast.

At the last possible second, Charlie spun to the left just as the iron pig left his hands. It wasn't much, but it was enough. The deadly doorstop sailed just enough off course to crash harmlessly into the wall half a metre from Housemama Rose's head.

"What on Earth are you *doing*, boy?" she yelled, shielding her face with her hands. "You nearly took my head clean off!"

"I'm so sorry!" Charlie said, rushing over to her and helping her to her feet. "It's just... I smelled cinnamon."

"Yes, from the toast, which is *ruined* now," she thundered, tucking errant wisps of grey hair back into the orderly sphere of her bun. "If you don't like toast, you should have just *said* something."

"It's not that, it's just... the cinnamon – when I smelled it, I thought it meant that you were..."

"A Mimic," she said, realisation dawning on her face.

Charlie nodded.

"Clever boy." Suddenly, the cabin began to sway, rocking back and forth in large arcs.

"What's going on?" Charlie asked, looking around nervously. The building had shifted so dramatically that he wondered if they were having an earthquake... but it didn't *feel* like an earthquake. The movement was too gentle.

"Relax, son," Housemama Rose said. "It's just the wind."

"The *wind* moved the whole cabin?"

"Oh, my," Housemama Rose said softly. "You don't know where we *are*, do you?"

"No, ma'am. It was dark when we got here and I went right to sleep."

She laughed then. It was big and round, like the rest of her. "Follow me," she said, walking to the door of the cabin. "You might find this... interesting."

It was more than interesting.

It was spectacular.

Built in and around a gigantic banyan tree, the Nightmare Academy was the world's most elaborate tree fort. Charlie stared at it in awe from the edge of a cliff that ran above the beach, overlooking the man-made marvel. Ramps and catwalks snaked up through branches so enormous, they could be mistaken for trees themselves. Huge sailing ships lay nestled on those branches, connected to one another by intricately woven nets and bridges. And they weren't *whole* ships either, Charlie noticed. They were mostly large *pieces* of ships: a hull from an old schooner, a stern from a pirate ship, a deck from an ancient warship, all of them scattered across the strong limbs like pieces of a jigsaw puzzle that fitted together in the most perfect and unexpected way.

Flags of various colours flapped in the breeze as water cascaded from somewhere high up above, splashing into troughs, which then snaked into and out of the various cabins and rooms, feeding the entire structure. And feeding, Charlie thought, was entirely accurate, because it was almost a *living thing*, the Nightmare Academy. It seemed too random and chaotic to have been built by sane human beings, and yet it clearly *had* been, cobbled together, piece by lunatic piece – a prow here, a plank there, a billowing sail up above. It was a glorious, crazy Meccano creation that shouldn't work, *couldn't* work really. But somehow it *did* – from the pirate mast at the very top to the collection of dinghies suspended at its base by large ropes.

"It's unbelievable," Charlie said, looking around with a wide smile.

"You get no argument from me," Mama Rose replied. "Long as I've been here, it still takes my breath away."

The warm tropical breeze ruffled the leaves of the palm trees that dotted the white sandy beach in front of the Academy. The water beyond was so clear that Charlie thought it was almost like looking into an aquarium. Fish darted playfully through the elaborate coral reef below, the sun reflecting off their scales in a rainbow of colour.

"It's the most beautiful place I've ever seen," Charlie

said. "Where in the world are we?"

"Safe," Mama Rose replied. "That's all you need to know right now. Although the island is vast and some of it is quite wild, the Academy itself is protected. It's a sanctuary from the monsters of the Nether." She glanced off in the distance to the dark jungle beyond. "That's not true of the rest of the island, you understand? Don't wander."

"No, ma'am. I mean, yes, ma'am. I mean, yes, Mama Rose."

She gave him a warm smile, then led him away from the cliff's edge, down a path and on to one of the waiting dinghies that lay suspended at the base of the banyan tree. "Hang on tight," she said. "We need to get you to orientation."

She jammed a lever that was nailed into the trunk and the dinghy shot upwards with blinding speed, pulled by a counterweight that sailed past them, heading towards the ground. Leaves and branches whipped by Charlie's face until the world's strangest lift finally came to an abrupt stop.

"Top floor, all out," Mama Rose said.

Charlie's stomach lurched when he saw how very high they were. The rest of the jungle spread out far beneath them. If he fell, he realised, it would take several seconds before he would even hit the *tops* of all the other trees.

He closed his eyes, took a breath to steady his nerves, then stepped out on to the deck of the pirate ship in front of him. There were several rows of worn wooden benches crowded with kids around his own age, all shifting uncomfortably, all looking distinctly out of place.

"Don't worry," Mama Rose said with a smile. "None of them knows what's about to happen either. You're in good company." She turned to go.

"You're leaving?" Charlie asked nervously.

"Of course. You don't need me here. Don't worry, you'll be *fine*." And with that, Mama Rose walked into another dinghy, hit a lever and dropped out of sight.

Reluctantly, Charlie took a seat on one of the benches.

He stared straight ahead, not looking anyone in the eye, trying desperately to avoid attention. But as much as he tried to shrink into the woodwork, he felt someone's eyes on *him*. He shifted uncomfortably, hoping whoever was staring at him would stop, but those unseen eyes still bored into him. Finally, he turned and saw a strange, gawky kid on the adjacent bench just staring at him with a wild smile.

The kid was tall for his age, with long, skinny arms and legs, big front teeth and a crazy shock of black hair. He looked for all the world like a puppet that had escaped its strings. He kept staring.

"What?" Charlie said finally.

"You're that kid," the stranger said. "The weirdo, right?"

"I don't think so," Charlie replied, wishing he'd never opened his mouth.

"Yeah, you are. You almost killed everyone at the Nightmare Division last night is what I heard."

"You heard about that *already?*" Charlie asked in disbelief.

"Uh, *yeah*," the kid said, and his cockeyed smile broadened. "Outrageous. Utterly outrageous. Total destruction. Beautiful, beautiful. My name's Theodore, by the way. Not Ted, Theodore. Last name Dagget. Not Dagger, Dagget, with a *t*. Got it?"

"Got it," Charlie said. The kid didn't offer to shake hands, so Charlie didn't either. "I'm Charlie," he said. "Charlie Benjamin."

"Excellent. I don't know anyone here. You're the first. I think we'll be best friends. What do you think?"

"Um," Charlie said. "I guess so." He didn't know what to say. No one had ever been so aggressively nice to him before.

"Good," Theodore declared. "Good to get that out of the way. So what do you think you're gonna be – Banisher or Nethermancer? Obviously, I'm gonna be a Banisher."

"How do you know?" Charlie asked.

"Come on, *look at me*," Theodore said, standing up. "I'm a guy! I'm built for combat!"

He didn't *look* built for combat, Charlie thought. In fact, he looked like a scarecrow in need of stuffing – all skin and bones and hard angles.

"Truth is, guys make the best Banishers," Theodore continued. "They don't like to tell you that. They try to keep the world PC – PC stands for political correctness – but Banishers are fighters, and fighting is in a guy's DNA – DNA stands for deoxyribonucleic acid. Girls, *chicks*, they're softer, more emotional. You want a portal, ask a girl. You want to drive a creature back to the Netherworld, that's my department. The GD – the guy department."

"*Please,*" a female voice said from behind them.

Charlie and Theodore turned to see a pretty, pony-tailed girl about their age doodling in a sketchbook. She was dressed casually in jeans and a white blouse with a little bit of pink embroidery at the top. She put her pen down and turned to Theodore. "The fact is, the *Nightmare Division's Guide to the Nether* says there are just as many female Banishers as males. The same is true of Nethermancers."

"Lies," Theodore countered. "Mistruths, exaggerations,

wishful thinking. Sorry. You lose."

"I do *not* lose," she said, starting to get angry. "Facts are facts."

"Facts are not, in fact, facts," Theodore shot back. "They are open to interpretation and, as such, are deeply suspicious and inherently unreliable."

"Do you even know what you're talking about?" she said.

"You do not want to get into a debate with me, miss," Theodore challenged. "I will eat your soul and spit it out. I will destroy you utterly."

"Oh, I'm *scared*," she said with a laugh.

"What a retort!" Theodore shot back. "Is that the totality of your linguistic arsenal? I bet you don't know a third of the words I do."

"Does anyone actually *like* you?"

"Of course," Theodore snapped. "Charlie here likes me. He's my best friend." He turned to Charlie. "Correct?"

"Um," Charlie said. "Look, we just met. I think we can *all* be friends. I'm Charlie." He extended his hand to the girl. She shook it.

"Nice to meet you, Charlie. I'm Violet."

"I see you like to draw," Charlie said, gesturing to her sketchpad.

She nodded. Her ponytail bounced playfully. "I'm on a dragon kick right now."

Charlie looked more closely at what she was drawing and saw a fantastically detailed sketch of a dragon with its long tail wrapped around a treasure hoard. "That's amazing," he said. "I wish I could draw like you."

"You could learn," Violet replied. "It just takes practice. I've spent a bunch of time studying the greats – Maitz, Whelan, Hickman, Targete."

"Who?" Theodore said.

"Well, I guess we finally found something you *don't* know. Don Maitz, Michael Whelan, Stephen Hickman, J P Targete – they're just some of the greats in the field of fantasy art, which I happen to love."

"Interesting," Theodore said, "that they're all *men*."

"Don't make me tell you about Rowena Morrell and Janny Wurts," Violet countered. "I will send you home crying."

"Oooh, now *I'm* scared."

And that's when they all heard a soft *pop!*

They turned to see a portal open at the stern of the ship. The Headmaster stepped through. The bright noonday sun made her tropical dress glow against her beautiful dark skin. With a casual wave of her hand, the portal disappeared behind her.

"Good morning," she said. "I am Headmaster Brazenhope."

"No way!" Theodore blurted, astonished. "The Headmaster's a chick!"

Without a word, the Headmaster waved her hand and a portal opened up in the deck beneath Theodore. He fell soundlessly into the Nether. With another wave, the portal closed shut behind him.

"Any other comments?" the Headmaster asked.

Everyone vigorously shook their heads.

"Good. Welcome to your first day at the Nightmare Academy. As you can see, it is a most unusual place, and yet I think it is entirely appropriate. I've always felt that dark and dangerous business is best learned in cheerful surroundings, and this island is very cheerful indeed. Don't you agree?"

The students nodded quickly.

"Now you may still be wondering why we have chosen to teach you in an environment so extraordinary – broken ships in trees, lifts fashioned from dinghies, plus the million and one outlandish nooks and crannies you have yet to discover. There are two reasons. The first I will tell you about now. The second you will discover when you are more capable of understanding it." She began to walk among the students as she continued. "The

Nightmare Academy is odd and unusual because it is the odd and unusual that stimulates the brain. There is nothing more poisonous to the imagination than sameness and repetition, and it is *imagination*, above all else, that we seek to nurture here. Why is that?"

It didn't seem like she was really asking a question, so no one ventured an answer, which was good, because she plunged forwards without waiting for one.

"It is imagination, ladies and gentlemen, that allows us to *do our jobs*, because it is imagination that allows us to access the *Gift*. Unfortunately, many of you, at least a third, will lose that powerful muscle during your stay here. It will atrophy and decay; it will wither and wilt. It happens to most people as they age, and it will, most assuredly and quite regrettably, happen to some of you as well. If that occurs, you will no longer have access to the Gift and you will cease to be able to use it to protect humanity from the creatures of the Nether."

She clapped her hands for emphasis. The students jumped.

"However," she continued, "loss of the Gift does not mean that you will cease to be valuable to our cause. Your training will be put to use. You will become *Facilitators* and you will accompany your Gifted comrades on their endeavours. Your task will not be an easy one. You will organise the missions and act as a liaison between the Nightmare Division and the agents in the field. Most of all, you will provide a third, calm voice when monsters are closing in and the Banisher and Nethermancer on your team are overwhelmed by their own responsibilities. Everyone here is important. Everyone here is critical."

Suddenly, Charlie realised that Pinch had said he was a Facilitator. Even though the Headmaster seemed to consider Facilitators equal members of the team, he wondered if it was difficult to have the Gift and then lose it. It seemed to explain a lot about Pinch's sour attitude and why he was such an advocate for having promising students Reduced – after all, if Pinch no longer had access to the Gift, why should anyone else?

"You are what's known as Noobs," the Headmaster continued. "That stands for 'Newbie'. Eventually, with training, you will advance to become Addys, meaning 'Adequate'. Finally, once you have demonstrated a significant amount of skill, you will be known as Leets, meaning 'Elite'. But for now you are Noobs, and Noobs you will remain for some time."

The Headmaster waved her hand. A portal opened in the middle of the air and Theodore fell through it, screaming, to land with a crash on his bench. The Headmaster dismissed the portal and continued as if nothing had happened. "As you may know, you will be trained as either a Nethermancer or a Banisher, depending on where your skill in the Gift lies."

"Hey, *lady*," Theodore blurted, obviously shaken. "Do you know that you put me into the Nether?"

"Yes," she said, and waved her hand.

Another portal opened beneath Theodore and he fell screaming, once again, into the Nether. The Headmaster dismissed the portal and continued.

"Today, we will determine which discipline your training will focus on. Some of you will leave here on the rocky road to becoming a Banisher; others will head down the prickly path to Nethermancy. They are both equally noble and equally difficult to master. We will begin with you, Ms Sweet. Are you ready?"

The gigantic banyan tree swayed gently in the wind. From somewhere off in the jungle, a bird screeched.

Suddenly, Violet jumped up. "You mean me?" she said.

"Your name is Violet Sweet, is it not?"

"Yes, Headmaster. I'm just not used to being called Ms Sweet, that's all."

"Get used to it," the Headmaster said. "I will address all of you as Mr and Ms from now on. One, because I think you secretly enjoy it. Two, because even though this appears to be just a school, we are, in fact, involved in quite serious business. We are training you to fight a war, ladies and gentlemen. A war that may involve casualties. If you are old enough to put your lives on the line in the service of a cause greater than yourselves, you are also old enough for me to treat you as adults and to expect adult behaviour from you. So, once again, I ask: are you ready, Ms Sweet?"

"Yes, Headmaster," she said.

"Excellent. Step forward."

As Violet walked towards her, the Headmaster waved her hand, opening a portal in mid-air. Once again, Theodore dropped through it and crashed into the benches below with a painful yelp.

"Welcome back, Mr Dagget. You've arrived just in time to watch Ms Sweet determine her future path."

"That really hurt," Theodore said.

"What a pity," the Headmaster replied. With another wave of her hand, a large portal snapped open beside her. Theodore flinched involuntarily. "Ladies and gentlemen, please follow Ms Sweet and me into the Nether. Her – and *your* – destinies await."

Moments later, after stepping through the portal, Charlie found himself standing in a field of fragrant yellow flowers that led to a cobalt blue lake as still and reflective as a mirror. The lake was nestled in a wooded glen of crisp-smelling pine trees and was surrounded on all sides by mountainous walls that rose so high, he couldn't see beyond them. The area was lovely and protected and, most of all, *hidden*.

"Wow," he murmured.

"Indeed," the Headmaster said as the last of the students stepped through the portal. With a quick wave of her hand, she dismissed it. "Though most of the Nether is dangerous and ugly, there are pockets, like this one, that defy expectation. We are, right now, in the 3rd ring. It is a mountainous region, full of creatures not to be trifled with, but this secret glen – tucked away on its eastern border – is uninhabited and always has been. There are no creatures of the Nether here... save one. One very *important* one."

The Headmaster turned to Violet.

"Ms Sweet, if you look carefully, you'll see that there are a series of stepping-stones that will take you out to the very centre of the lake."

Violet looked and saw a line of white stones that led to a small rock in the middle. "I see them," she said.

"Excellent. You are to walk to the centre of the lake and declare yourself. You will shout out either 'I am a

Banisher!' or 'I am a Nethermancer!'"

"But how do I pick which one?" she asked. "I have no idea what I am."

"Simply say what you feel," the Headmaster answered. "Say what you think is *true*."

"OK," Violet said. "And what will happen then?"

"Then," the Headmaster replied with a twinkle in her eye, "we will discover if you are *correct*. Go on, please." She gestured to the lake.

With a nervous glance at the rest of the students, Violet walked to the water's edge. The stepping-stones that broke the surface were small and uneven and she had to steady herself more than once as she leaped across them, heading to the very centre of the lake. After arriving on the white, weathered rock in the middle, she looked down into the dark water, searching for movement, for any sign of something *alive* in there, but the water was as still as glass and reflected the sheer mountain walls surrounding them, making it impossible to see through.

"Let's go, Ms Sweet," the Headmaster yelled. "Declare yourself!"

As much as Violet had argued with Theodore that girls could be Banishers just as well as guys, she knew in her heart that her destiny lay down a different path.

"*I am a Nethermancer!*" she shouted.

Her words echoed off the still lake and reverberated from the walls of the canyon with shocking intensity, startling her. Soon the echoes faded and, once again, there was silence. Violet glanced around uncomfortably at the dark water. It was still and glassy.

"Now what?" she asked.

And that was when a giant trout leaped from the lake in an explosion of water. It was the size of a school bus, this trout, and its glistening skin was speckled with spots of red and grey and green. It arced across the rock that Violet stood on, scooped her into its wide, clammy mouth and crashed back into the cold water on the far side, instantly disappearing from view. The lake rocked and rippled violently as the students stared in shock.

Violet and the giant trout that had swallowed her were gone.

"Wha... what was *that*?" Theodore finally gasped, his jaw hanging open like a broken hinge.

"That," the Headmaster replied, "was the Trout of Truth."

CHAPTER EIGHT
THE TROUT
OF TRUTH

"Where is she?" Charlie asked with growing panic. "Where's Violet?! *It's not just gonna eat her, is it?*"

Just then, the Trout burst from the water near the flowery bank and, with a wet, gurgling sound, it spat Violet from its mouth. She flew through the air, spinning and tumbling like a rag doll, before finally landing in a tangled clump of arms and legs at the Headmaster's feet. The Trout slipped back under the water and was soon gone from view.

Charlie ran towards Violet and helped her to her feet. "Are you OK?" he asked.

"I... I don't know," she said shakily, wiping slime and algae from her face. She was absolutely drenched in the disgusting ooze.

"Congratulations, Ms Sweet," the Headmaster said. "You are a Banisher."

"How do you know?" Violet asked, squeezing goo from her long hair.

"Because, of all the creatures in the Nether, only the Trout is able to precisely determine whether or not someone is telling the truth. And, as you have just witnessed, it absolutely will not tolerate an *untruth* on its lake. It will remove the source of the untruth immediately."

"But I didn't lie," Violet protested.

"No, not knowingly," the Headmaster said. "You claimed that you were a Nethermancer and I'm sure you believed in your heart that you were, but the Trout has found that to be untrue. Consequently, we know that if you are not a Nethermancer, then you must be a Banisher."

"But are you sure the Trout is always right?" Violet asked. "I'm not much of a fighter."

"You will be," the Headmaster assured her. "The Trout has never been wrong." She turned to another student. "Mr Ramirez, please step out to the centre of the lake. Let's see what the future holds for you."

Alejandro Ramirez, a stocky twelve-year-old, made his way out to the rock. "I am... a Nethermancer," he said softly, glancing around nervously at the still water.

There was no response from the Trout.

"Excellent, Mr Ramirez," the Headmaster said.

"Seeing as how you were not swallowed alive, what you said must have been the truth, although I would have appreciated a little more forcefulness from your declaration. Congratulations, you are our first Nethermancer of the day." As Alejandro rushed back to the group, clearly thankful that he didn't have to get swallowed by the Trout, the Headmaster turned to another kid. "Mr Favrutti, step up."

It went on like this for almost an hour.

Nearly twenty kids declared themselves to the Trout and roughly half of them were right. The other half were immediately swallowed by the giant fish and then spat up upon the shore like a discarded wad of gum. Charlie was somewhat surprised to discover that Violet had been correct when she said that the job of Banisher was evenly split between boys and girls. The same was true of Nethermancers – neither job seemed to favour one sex over the other.

Finally, it was Theodore's turn to face the Trout. "Yes!" he said, and nearly sprinted up to the Headmaster. "My dad was a Banisher. Did you know that?"

She nodded. "I remember your father. He was extremely bright and often very annoying. You remind me of him. How is he?"

"Good, I guess," Theodore said. "He's off somewhere

fighting Nethercreatures. He's not allowed to tell us where. It's a black op. Op is short for *operation*, and a black op means—"

"I know what it means," the Headmaster interrupted. "Let's get on with it, shall we?"

"Definitely," Theodore said. "I can't wait for my dad to come back from the black op so I can tell him I'm going to be a Banisher, just like him." He quickly skipped across the stones to stand on the rock in the very centre of the lake. He cleared his throat and shouted as loudly and proudly as he could, "*I am a Banisher!*"

The water was still.

"See," Theodore said, turning to the shore. "Told you."

And that was when the Trout leaped from the lake and swallowed Theodore whole. Moments later, he found himself flying through the air and landing in an ungraceful clump in front of the Headmaster.

"I'm sorry, Mr Dagget," she said as Theodore struggled to his feet, shaky as a newborn fawn. "You are not a Banisher. The Trout has shown us that you are a Nethermancer."

"Wrong," Theodore said, spitting slime from his mouth.

"Excuse me?" The Headmaster replied, raising a single eyebrow.

"No offence, ma'am, but the Trout is wrong. Definitely wrong. No way I'm a Nethermancer."

"The Trout is *never* wrong," the Headmaster shot back. "It is *you* who are wrong, Mr Dagget."

"Look, I'm not saying the Trout *intentionally* screwed up. I'm just saying it made a mistake. Everyone makes mistakes. It can't be right *every* time, right? It's just a dumb fish."

"Well, if you're so certain," the Headmaster replied, "you're welcome to try again."

"Definitely," Theodore said, and stomped back out to the middle of the lake. He arched his back and shouted to the sky, "I am a Banisher!"

It took less than twenty seconds for the Trout to leap out of the water, swallow him and spit him back up on shore. Once again, Theodore struggled to his feet.

"There's something wrong with that Trout," he said. "Maybe it's sick."

"The Trout is not sick," the Headmaster replied.

"Then maybe it's old or tired or something. I'm telling you, I can't be a Nethermancer. It's an IS – an impossible situation! Every guy in my family was a Banisher!"

"I'm sorry," the Headmaster said, clearly beginning to lose her patience. "I know you wanted to be a Banisher, but you are, in fact, a Nethermancer."

"No," Theodore said. "That Trout is screwed up, plain and simple. You have a defective Truth Trout!"

"It has spoken *twice*."

"*Then it's been wrong two times!* Maybe it just needs one more chance to realise I'm right." And, with that, he turned and sprinted back to the centre of the lake. "I am a Banisher!" he shouted, his words echoing loudly across the canyon walls.

The Trout jumped from the lake and swallowed him instantly.

Charlie turned to Violet. "How many times do you think he's going to do this before he gives up?"

"Four," she said without hesitation.

"I think five," Charlie replied.

Incredibly, it took *seven*.

Seven times Theodore was swallowed by the Trout of Truth before, reeking of fish and covered in slime, he finally gave up – but not happily.

"Stupid Trout," he said, kicking at the flowers on shore as he struggled once again to his feet.

"Mr Dagget," the Headmaster said with a touch of weariness, "just accept that you are a Nethermancer. It is an extremely honourable vocation, no more or less noble than being a Banisher, and you may as well start getting used to it."

"I'll *never* get used to it," Theodore said as he stomped off angrily, grumbling about "unfair trout" and "dumb fish" and "just one more chance".

The Headmaster turned to the rest of the students. "That concludes orientation," she said. "We will now return to the Nightmare Academy and you will meet Housemistress Rose to get your timetable and syllabus."

"Headmaster?" Charlie said, raising his hand. "I don't mean to interrupt, but I haven't had my turn yet."

"Ah, Mr Benjamin. I believe your adventures the previous night have already shown us your path. Anyone able to create a portal to the Inner Circle is clearly a Nethermancer. A Banisher would not have the aptitude to do such a thing."

"Oh, OK," Charlie said.

"Hey!" Alejandro Ramirez yelled. "All the rest of us had to face the Trout. Why does he get off so easy?"

"Because, as I said, we already *know* his path," the Headmaster replied.

"I guess. It just doesn't seem *fair*," he moaned.

"He's right," Charlie said, not wanting to set himself apart from the group. "I should take a turn."

Moments later, Charlie stood on the rock in the middle of the lake. He could feel a chill breeze emanating from the cold water, which seemed to be quite deep as well – how else could it contain a creature as large as the Trout of Truth?

Charlie closed his eyes, took a breath and finally shouted, "I am a Nethermancer!"

As expected, there was no movement from the Trout. Charlie had spoken the truth. He breathed a sigh of relief, then started walking back towards the shore. "You were right," he called out to the Headmaster as he skipped from one stone to the next. "I'm not a Banisher."

As soon as he said it, the Trout exploded from the water and clamped its clammy lips around Charlie, sealing him in stinking, wet darkness. He was thrown violently around the slimy insides of the ancient creature as it crashed back into the water, swimming to shore. Moments later, daylight blinded Charlie as the Trout spat him out of its innards. He twirled and tumbled high into the air before finally slamming back down on to the hard ground of the field.

The students stared in amazement.

"Are you OK?" Violet asked, rushing to him.

"Yeah," Charlie said, getting to his feet. "I just wasn't expecting it, that's all."

"Because it doesn't make any sense!" Theodore shouted. "See, I told you that Trout's gone wacko! It agreed with him when he said he was a Nethermancer, but it called him a liar when he said he wasn't a Banisher. That's definitely wrong – you can't be a Nethermancer *and* a Banisher!"

"That's true," the Headmaster said quietly. "Unless you're a *Double-Threat*."

The students glanced at one another.

"What's that?" Violet asked.

"A person who can both Banish *and* Nethermance. They're quite rare actually – maybe one born every twenty or thirty years." The Headmaster turned to Charlie. "You certainly are full of surprises, Mr Benjamin."

Charlie was speechless.

One born every twenty or thirty years.

Most people would have been flattered to be something so special, but to Charlie, it sounded as if she were talking about some mutant, two-headed calf or a freakish eel that could walk on land. He had always felt like an outcast. Now he felt like an outcast times two.

"Outrageous!" Theodore exclaimed. "Charlie the Double-Threat! Charlie the DT!"

"Don't call me that," Charlie muttered. He was

discovering that Theodore could usually be counted on to be enthusiastic about the wrong things.

"Hey, Headmaster," Theodore continued. "What about you? Are you one of those Double-Threats? Are you a DT?"

"Don't call me that," she said. "And to answer your question, yes, I am what's known as a Double-Threat, but it's not nearly as grand a thing as it seems. It's true that I can both Banish and Nethermance, but not at the same time. They are entirely different skills and each of them requires such focus and concentration that it is simply impossible to perform both tasks at once."

"Oh," Theodore said, disappointed. "That's like having an Aston Martin and a Ferrari – they're nice, but you can only drive one at a time. What's the point?"

"The point," she said, "is that variety is the spice of life and I prefer my life *very* spicy." She then created a portal that opened back on to the top deck of the Nightmare Academy. "We've finished for today. Class dismissed."

Minutes later, having returned to the Academy, Charlie walked down one of the many ramps that wrapped around its gigantic trunk as Theodore bounded alongside, babbling excitedly. "Sure it may be *useless*," he said, "but it's *rare*. That's so excellent. Did you hear the Headmaster? One born every twenty or thirty *years*. We're all unusual – I mean the Gift only affects like two per cent of the population – but you, my friend, you are a *mutant*. My best friend is a *freak*!"

"Will you *stop* that already," Violet said, walking up between them. "It's obvious you're making Charlie uncomfortable."

"No, I'm not, Miss Busybody. Are you uncomfortable, Charlie? Am I, in any way, shape or form, making you uncomfortable?"

"I guess not," Charlie said, clearly uncomfortable.

"See," Theodore crowed triumphantly, "we're *men*. We're not as weepy and emotional as you mere girls."

Violet turned to Charlie. "You're really not going to tell him how you feel?"

Charlie *wanted* to say something, to tell Theodore that he'd spent his entire life feeling like an outcast but now that he was in a place full of kids *just like him*, the last thing he wanted was to hear how different he was. But he just couldn't bring himself to do it. Theodore, odd as he was, was becoming a real friend, and Charlie was desperate not to jeopardise that.

"I'm fine," Charlie said to Violet. "Really."

"Ugh! Well, if you're not going to stick up for yourself, I'm certainly not going to do it for you." She pushed past the two of them, heading down the ramp.

"I stick up for myself," Charlie lamely called after her, but by then, she was gone.

"There he is," an angry voice suddenly chimed out from behind them. "The psycho who almost destroyed the Nightmare Division!"

CHAPTER NINE
THE MEANING OF POGD

Charlie and Theodore turned to see a tall girl about fifteen years old walking towards them down the ramp. She was breathtakingly beautiful. Her blonde hair was long and looked like it had been carefully styled. In fact, everything about her was carefully done – from her carefully applied make-up to her carefully chosen outfit, which was far more fashionable than anything else Charlie had seen at the Nightmare Academy.

Following behind her like an eager dog on a lead was a good-looking teenage boy about her age. Broad and muscular, with blond hair and blue eyes, his only weakness, as far as Charlie could tell, was that he was trying desperately to grow a moustache with no real success.

"You're that Charlie Benjamin, right?" the girl asked.

"I guess so," Charlie replied.

Conflicting emotions warred inside him. She was clearly getting ready to attack him in some way and he knew he should prepare to defend himself, but she was so pretty that it nearly made him dizzy. He had never had a girlfriend, never gone on a date, never even held a girl's *hand*, but now he was getting the undivided attention of one of the most beautiful girls he had ever seen.

Unfortunately, it was only because she clearly hated him.

"I'm Brooke Brighton," she said with a tone that suggested he should already know who she was. "I'm a Facilitator. And this is my boyfriend, Geoff Lench." She threw a quick backwards glance in his direction. "He's a Facilitator too."

Geoff leaned towards Charlie, stroking his embryonic moustache as if it made him seem years older than he was. It didn't. "We heard you almost let a Named into the middle of the High Council chamber last night – Noob."

"I didn't mean to," Charlie replied weakly.

"Didn't *mean* to?" Brooke countered, stepping closer. "Is that what you said to Director Drake after you almost killed everyone? That you didn't *mean* to?"

A clear winner was emerging in the emotional battle raging inside Charlie. Brooke was certainly pretty –

beautiful in fact – but the attraction he felt towards her was quickly giving way to anger over the way she was treating him.

"If *I* was your Facilitator," she continued, "I'd see to it that you got put on probation pending an investigation under Article 36 of the ND bylaws – Drake edition. In fact, I'd see to it that you were *Reduced.* What do you think of that?"

"I think," Charlie said, struggling to find a way to respond to something so unbelievably cruel, "that you're just mad at me because I still have the Gift and you lost it. I mean, that *is* why you're a Facilitator, isn't it?"

Charlie heard several sharp intakes of breath as the other kids on the ramp looked around nervously. Clearly, he had crossed some kind of line.

"What did you say to me?" Brooke asked, her voice hardly more than a whisper.

"I'm just wondering *why* you lost it," Charlie continued, bracing himself. "The Gift, I mean. It probably wasn't your fault. Did you get too interested in clothes? Or TV? Or *boys*?"

Suddenly, Geoff snatched him by the front of his shirt and yanked him so close that Charlie could smell the mint gum he chewed. "You watch how you talk to her, you miserable little Noob, or I'll toss you off the top of the

Academy just to see if you can fly. Got me?"

But before Charlie could answer, Theodore took off his glasses. "Hold these," he said.

"Why?" Charlie asked, taking them.

Without answering, Theodore turned and, out of nowhere, took a wild, loping swing at Geoff. He connected solidly with the side of his tanned face, dropping him to his knees on the hard wood of the ramp. The gum sailed from his mouth like a stray tooth.

"No fair!" Brooke yelled. "You sucker-punched him, you little cheat!"

Theodore was now full of adrenaline. His herky-jerky scarecrow features were flushed with excitement. "And I'll do it again and again if you mess with Charlie Benjamin! I will destroy you! Both of you! I will eat your souls and feast on your bones! I will—"

But before he could utter the next meaningless threat, Geoff leaped at him, knocking him backwards into the trunk of the giant banyan tree. Even though Theodore got the first shot, Geoff was thirty centimetres taller and had twice his weight, all of it muscle. He pounded Theodore relentlessly with blow after crushing blow.

"Stop it!" Charlie yelled. "You're really hurting him!"

"Shut up, Noob," Geoff snarled. "You're next."

"GEOFF LENCH, KNOCK IT OFF RIGHT THIS

SECOND!" a voice bellowed from the end of the ramp.

Charlie turned and was shocked to see that the voice belonged to Mama Rose. She barrelled towards them like a wrecking ball, and students who didn't get out of the way quickly enough were knocked aside like pins in a bowling alley.

"He started it," Geoff said defensively, backing up. "He swung first."

"He may have swung first, but I saw what happened, and he didn't start it," Mama Rose replied. "This isn't the first trouble you've got into this year, Geoff Lench. Heck, it's not even the first trouble you got into this *week*."

"But I have to be able to defend myself," he protested.

"*Please*," Mama Rose said dismissively. "Look at the boy. He's a toothpick. Do you remember what happened the last time you broke the rules and got yourself hauled in front of the Headmaster?"

"She sent me into the Nether," Geoff said sheepishly.

"What ring in the Nether?"

"The 2nd ring."

"And what happened to you while you were there?"

Geoff looked around uncomfortably. "A Nethersnapper bit my big toe off."

"*Bit off your big toe, didn't it?*" Mama Rose bellowed. "And did that big toe grow back, Geoff Lench?"

"No."

"*Of course not,* because human big toes are not like lizard tails! They do not grow back! Now, unless you'd like to take another trip into the Nether – maybe the 3rd ring this time, where the creatures might have a taste for something softer and more delicate than a big toe – I suggest you get out of here and leave these Noobs alone."

"Yes, Mama Rose," Geoff said, pale now with the thought of exactly *what* soft and delicate bits she was referring to. He raced off down the ramp.

"And you, Little Miss Sunshine," Mama Rose said, spinning towards Brooke. "I greatly, *sincerely* recommend that you stay far away from Charlie Benjamin."

"I didn't do anything," Brooke replied innocently. "It was Geoff who punched him, not me."

"Who do you think you're talking to, missy?" Mama Rose shot back. "That dumb lunk is no better than a puppet you yank around with all your little flirty bits. He's too stupid to know how stupid he is. *Now get outta here.*"

Scowling, Brooke Brighton walked off down the gangplank as Charlie helped Theodore to his feet. His nose was bloody and his upper lip was already growing fat.

"You know where the infirmary is, boy?" Mama Rose asked.

"Yeah," Theodore said, slurring. "But I'm OK."

"No, you're not OK. You look about as good as a pig in a woodchipper. Now, you're gonna go to the infirmary and then you're gonna head to your first class – Neophyte Nethermancy starts in three hours. And, listen to me closely, boy." Mama Rose leaned in only centimetres from his face. "The next time you throw a punch, follow through with your body. You swing like a girl."

And with that, Mama Rose stalked off, leaving startled students in her wake.

The infirmary was a large tent that had been constructed on a platform about midway up the trunk of the banyan tree. The tent itself was made of coarse, ivory-coloured fabric from the sails of a ship. It rippled slightly in the breeze. Inside, Theodore held an ice pack to his fat lip as a nurse put antibiotic cream on his bruises. His face had swollen slightly, which, oddly enough, made him look more healthy – he didn't seem quite so skeletal.

"Why did you do it?" Charlie asked. "He was twice as big as you."

"He was messing with you," Theodore said, slurring, as if that was answer enough.

"Well, let me fight my own battles next time, OK?" Charlie said. "It's not like I'm totally helpless."

Theodore shrugged. "Can't make any promises. When my best friend is in danger, my fists take on a mind of their own. They become forces of destruction. Weapons of death."

"You're good to go," the nurse said, screwing the cap back on the ointment. "And try to keep those weapons of death locked up until you heal a little bit," she added with a wry smile.

"I'll do my best," Theodore said grudgingly, handing her back the ice pack. "But sometimes my fists start talking before my feet start walking – that's just the way I roll."

Charlie was astonished that Theodore could be so confident, so incredibly *sure* of himself. As much as Charlie had desperately wanted to get out of the house and be around kids his own age, now that he was reminded how truly mean some of them could be, he was filled with self-doubt. His parents might have been smothering and overprotective, but they had loved him totally. And there had been moments of real joy. Charlie suddenly grinned at the memory of the trip to the local amusement park they had all taken on his last birthday. His mum, of course, had refused to go anywhere near the roller coasters – she called them "puke machines" – but he and his father rode them with a manic glee.

"The Benjamin men face their fears!" Barrington shouted triumphantly during the car's long, slow climb before its first delicious plunge. "The Benjamin men are not afraid!" And then they raised their hands high in the air and the coaster plummeted and they screamed together in delightful terror.

A stabbing pang of homesickness shot through Charlie.

"You OK?" Theodore asked, staring at him with concern.

"I'm fine," Charlie said, trying his best to snap out of it. "Just remembering something. I have to run actually. Beginning Banishing starts in a few minutes."

"I wish I could go," Theodore moaned. "But I have to wait for stupid Nethermancy."

"I'll be there too, after I finish my first class."

"Double-Threat means double the work, huh?" Theodore said with a smile.

"Looks that way."

"Well, good luck. I'm sure I'll be joining you in Banishing soon enough – after the Headmaster realises a tragic mistake has been made, I mean."

Charlie nodded supportively. "I'll try my best to remember what happens so I can fill you in when the time comes. See you later."

And with that, he headed off to his first class in the Nightmare Academy.

Beginning Banishing took place in an arena that had been carved out of the limestone interior of a cave near the coastline, far away from the Academy itself. At the centre of the arena was a round, sandy pit, surrounded by stone bleachers that rose upwards like a coliseum, giving the spectators a clear view of what was happening below. The place felt so ancient that Charlie imagined Roman gladiators battling it out in that pit long ago.

"There you are," a familiar voice said. Charlie turned to see Violet, sitting on one of the stone benches with about fifteen other kids, drawing on her sketchpad. "I heard you got into a fight."

"Well, technically, *Theodore* did," Charlie said, walking over to her. "At least he was the one throwing punches and getting beaten up."

"He loves that stuff, doesn't he?"

"I don't know if he loves it, but his dad is a Banisher – maybe it's just in his blood. The *desire* to fight, I mean, not the ability."

Violet leaned in confidentially. "Don't you dare tell him this, but he really should be here instead of me.

I have no interest in fighting, *none*... I'd rather just draw."

"What are you working on?"

She held up her drawing. It was a detailed sketch of a dragon in flight, clutching an egg in its talons as it breathed fire at another dragon in furious pursuit. "I call it *The Egg Thief*. This dragon has stolen the egg of the mama dragon behind it and she's *mad*. What do you think?"

"It's amazing. It looks absolutely real – for something that's not real, I mean."

"Thanks, but I have a long way to go before I can compete with the pros," she said with a dismissive wave, clearly happy for the compliment all the same.

Suddenly, the large wooden doors leading into the pit below were flung open and Rex strode through, cowboy hat confidently cocked on his head, lasso and short sword hanging at his hip. "All right, let's get on with this," he said to the assembled students scattered across the stone bleachers. "Last one in the pit gets forty lashes."

The students scrambled down the stone steps and into the arena; no one wanted to be last on the first day.

Rex surveyed them sceptically. "So, you're the future Wranglers of the ND, huh?" He shook his head sadly. "We're in big trouble."

"Sir?" Violet asked.

"I just go by Rex. What?"

"You called us 'Wranglers'. I thought we were Banishers."

"Wranglers, Banishers, you say po-tay-to, I say po-tah-to. It doesn't matter. Look, bottom line – I don't want to be here. I'm a field agent, not a babysitter for wet-behind-the-ear Noobs, got it?"

Everyone nodded.

"That said," Rex continued, "here I am and here I'll stay till some ugly politics are ironed out, so we may as well all make the best of it. Sooner we get started, sooner we get done, so let's rock and roll. Who knows what POGD stands for?"

The students were silent.

"No one, huh?" Rex said, baffled. "Not a single one of you knows the most basic rule of Banishing? Wow. OK, POGD stands for 'point of greatest dark'. Wish I had a blackboard or something so I could write that down. Anyway, what it means is that a Nethercritter – Nether*creature* if you want the hundred per cent correct terminology, *Miss Only One Way to Call Something*."

He fixed Violet with a stare. She blushed furiously.

"Anyway," he continued, "what it means is that your basic bogeyman will almost *always* seek the darkest place around after it portals into our world. Because they're usually coming in through a nightmare and because nightmares usually happen in bed, eighty per cent of the time your basic Nethercritter is gonna be found in the darkest place in a kid's bedroom. Any thoughts what those places might be?"

A short boy of Native American descent raised his hand tentatively. "Yeah?" Rex said, pointing to him.

"Under the bed?" the boy suggested.

"Under the bed, of course! You get a gold star – not really, but you know what I mean. How many times have we heard about 'the creature under the bed'? Well, that's because, half the dang time, *that's where they hide*! Name another place."

Several students, emboldened by the first kid's success, raised their hands. Rex pointed to the youngest of them, a little, round-faced girl in pigtails.

"You – Pigtails. Speak."

"In the wardrobe," she said with a gulp.

"In the dang wardrobe, thank you!" Rex bellowed. "Creature under the bed, bogeyman in the wardrobe, ghost in the attic – we hear about these things all the time *because they're true*. So when you're first called to investigate a house where there's been a suspected portalling – you instantly look for the *what*?"

"The point of greatest dark," the class shouted back at him.

"My God, there's hope for you yet," Rex said with a hint of a smile. "But before we start giving each other high fives, let's get down to the business of Banishing."

He walked over to a rough wooden table, on top of which was a variety of used-looking weapons – beaten-up swords, chipped axes, maces with broken handles. It wasn't very inspiring.

"Now I know this stuff looks like junk, and that's because it *is*, but you don't deserve better, least not until you know what to do with a *real* weapon. Even though they're crap, they're still a dang sight more useful than a normal weapon, least for our purposes anyway. See, these were all created from materials in the Nether – iron ore, rope, that kind of stuff – so they'll respond to people with the Gift. Now go ahead and grab yourself one."

The students rushed to the table. Violet picked a small dagger because it seemed the least imposing of the choices. Duct tape was wrapped around the hilt, presumably to keep it from falling apart. It glowed dimly blue in her grasp.

Charlie gravitated to a long, thin rapier. It lacked the heft of a sword but what it missed in weight, it made up for in speed. He whipped it around wildly, leaving a trail of sparkly blue mist in the air. The rest of his classmates grabbed the remaining weapons – a mace, several swords, even a spear. After all the budding Banishers had made their selections, there was only a strange pile of junk left on the wooden table – a metal chain, a crowbar, a torch, a bottle opener.

"No one wants the bottle opener, huh?" Rex said. "You sure? Never know when you might need a good bottle opener."

There were no takers. The students, predictably, were too enamoured with the more obviously lethal weapons that they had chosen. "En garde!" Charlie said, happily challenging another boy to a duel. They started play-fighting, and soon the other kids joined in. Swords clanged against maces, axes clattered against pole-arms.

"Whoa, whoa, whoa," Rex yelled. "Put those things down before you hack off a nose or chop off a leg. This ain't nursery school, this is serious business."

Reluctantly, they lowered their weapons.

"Now let's see how you do against your first Nethercritter." The large wooden doors that led to the arena suddenly opened and a Netherstalker the size of a pickup truck crept into the room on its eight giant spider legs. The students gasped and stepped back – no one was prepared for something like this their first time out.

"Good luck," Rex said with a grin, and walked towards the back of the arena. As he passed by Charlie, he whispered, "By the way, kid, the answer is four."

"The answer to what?" Charlie asked, but by then Rex had passed him by.

As the Netherstalker approached, the class timidly held their cheap weapons in front of them, illuminating the ferocious beast in a weak blue light. The Netherstalker stared at them with its dark spider eyes... then it threw back its head and laughed.

"And what do you think you're doing?" it said with amusement.

CHAPTER TEN
THE TRANSFORMING SNARK

"**W**hat... what did it say?" the girl in pigtails asked, bewildered.

"*It*," the Netherstalker answered with particular emphasis, "said 'And what do you think you're doing?' Probably because *it* was amused to see a class of Noobs actually raising weapons to *it*."

Rex walked back up.

"*It* has a name, by the way," he said, clapping the creature affectionately on one of its hairy legs. "This is Professor Xixclix and he's been the Academy's Beastmaster since I was a Noob. How you doing, Xix?"

"Not bad," the creature said with a grin. "Except it seems like I keep getting older and they don't."

"Well, age catches up with even the best of us," Rex replied warmly, then turned to the class. "Here's your next lesson: all creatures from the Nether are not mindless, slobbering beasts. Some of 'em are pretty smart. And, in the case of old Xix here, at least one of them has switched sides and agreed to help us out. Xix, cos of his rather special experience, handles all the creatures from the Nether that we'll be using in our training."

"Quite right," Xix said, scuttling forwards. The students instinctively took a step back. "Now you all know I am a Netherstalker, but who can tell me what *Class* I am?"

There was silence then, until Charlie suddenly remembered what Rex had told him. *The answer is four.*

"Four!" he shouted.

"Exactly," Xix said. "To tell the Class of a Netherstalker, you need only count the eye stalks." Charlie looked and saw that Xix did, in fact, have four eye stalks. "Here's another question," he continued. "As a creature from the Nether ages, do they rise in Class or do they stay the same Class their entire lives?"

Violet tentatively raised her hand.

"You, young Banisher," Xix said, pointing to her with a hairy leg.

"They rise in Class?" she ventured.

"Quite right," Xix said with a nod. "And how did you come to that conclusion?"

"Because I noticed you have a fifth eye stalk just beginning to bud, which would mean that you're growing into a Class 5."

"Excellent!" Xix said. "Very observant. When I first joined the Nightmare Academy, I was a Class 3. Several years ago, I advanced to a Class 4. Soon I will be a Class 5. You have good eyes, young Banisher."

"Thank you," Violet said, blushing slightly.

"Now just sit tight and I'll be back momentarily with your first challenge." He scuttled out of the arena through the large wooden doors.

"While we wait," Rex said, stepping forwards, "I'd like you to meet Kyoko. She's a Leet Nethermancer who will be helping us out today by making a portal."

A tall, seventeen-year-old Asian girl stepped down from the viewing gallery. Her long black hair hung straight against her porcelain skin. "Hey, everyone," she said with a smile. "You want the portal now, Professor?"

"Nah, you can open it soon as Xix unveils the critter these Noobs will be Banishing – and call me Rex."

"OK," she said, giggling a little.

She has a crush on him, Charlie thought with some amusement.

Just then Xix returned carrying a wriggling bag of spider silk. It looked like a cocoon. He placed it on the sandy arena floor. "I present to you a Class-1 Ectobog," he said, then quickly sliced through the spider silk to reveal the creature inside.

A green blob the size of a Dobermann slithered out. It seemed to have the consistency of a jellyfish and, in the middle, Charlie could see the remains of its last meal. There were small bones in there, a belt buckle and something that looked suspiciously like an iPod.

"Charlie, you're up," Rex said, hitching a thumb in his direction.

"Me?" Charlie replied, alarmed. "What do I do?"

"Banish it into the portal, course," Rex answered casually, then turned to Kyoko. "Fire one up, if you don't mind."

Kyoko closed her eyes and concentrated fiercely. Her body glowed with electric purple flame and, after several seconds, she opened a small portal in the middle of the arena.

"Um," Charlie said, unsure.

"Come on, kid – it ain't gonna Banish itself," Rex teased.

Charlie tentatively crept towards the Ectobog, holding his rapier out in front of him, probing delicately like a blind man with a walking stick. As he neared the creature, the blue glow of the rapier intensified.

"See, that blue glow gets brighter the nearer you get to a Nethercritter," Rex explained. "In fact, sometimes you can use it to tell if a baddie is sneaking up on you."

The class nodded, but Charlie didn't hear a word; he was focused on the pile of goo in front of him. As he got to within a couple of metres of the Ectobog, it seemed to become aware of him and oozed slowly in his direction, its skin shimmering like an oil slick after a rainstorm.

"Now what?" Charlie asked.

"How should I know?" Rex replied with a grin. "You're the Banisher."

"Great..." Charlie mumbled, then turned back to the Ectobog. The closer it got to him, the faster it moved. "Get back!" he shouted as he brought his rapier whistling down. To his amazement, he sliced the Ectobog neatly in two. "Cool!" he said after realising what he'd done.

The class cheered and applauded and Charlie felt a warm rush of success and approval. "Go Charlie!" Violet shouted.

Charlie turned and took a stage bow.

As he did, something strange happened behind him. The two halves of the Ectobog quivered like jelly, then began to grow, until they formed two separate Ectobogs, each one identical in size to the original.

Both Ectobogs oozed towards Charlie.

"Look out!" Violet yelled.

Charlie turned and saw the creatures sliming towards him. "What do I do?" he shouted. "When you attack, it makes two of them!"

"Gee, that's a problem," Rex replied, slightly amused.

One of the Ectobogs reached Charlie's foot. It quickly oozed up his leg and Charlie could feel it inside his jeans. It was cold and clammy, like an oyster.

"It's got me!" he yelled and, purely by instinct, he sliced at it again with his rapier. It split cleanly in two. After a moment, the two halves quivered, then each one quickly grew to full size. Immediately, *both* Ectobogs swarmed up towards Charlie's belly as the third one caught up and joined them.

Now he had *three* on him.

"Uh-oh," Rex said casually. "Somebody better do something. This could get ugly."

The kids in the class glanced at one another nervously. No one knew *what* to do. How do you defeat something that gets stronger as you attack it?

"Wait..." Violet said suddenly.

She threw down her dagger and raced back to the weapons table. Quickly, she dug through the remaining pile of junk, grabbed the torch and turned it on. Bright white light shot from the bulb in a focused beam, while the torch itself glowed a brilliant blue. She pointed it at the Ectobogs, which were now creeping up Charlie's chest, heading towards his face.

"Get off him!" she yelled.

The Ectobogs reacted to the light as if stung. They quickly slithered off Charlie and retreated. Violet pressed forwards, using the beam of light to herd them towards the open portal.

"Go on!" she shouted. "Get out of here!"

With one last sweep of the torch, the Ectobogs retreated into the portal.

"Should I close it?" Kyoko asked, purple flames flickering across her.

"Yes, please," Violet answered, her heart hammering in her chest.

With a wave of her hand, Kyoko closed the portal, sealing the Ectobogs in the Nether. There was silence then, broken finally by the sound of one person clapping. Violet turned to see Rex giving her a round of applause.

"And that's how you do *that*," he said. "What made you think to use the torch?"

"Well, what you said earlier about the point of greatest dark – that creatures from the Nether don't like the light."

"Exactly," Rex said, bounding towards her. "See, Banishing's not all about fighting and strength, it's mostly about *thinking*. 'Using your noodle', as my momma used to say. The Wrangler that can keep her head and think outside of the box is the one who'll live to Banish another day. Congrats, kid."

He shot Violet a friendly wink.

Violet left the class on a real high. "Maybe I *can* do this," she said as they walked along the crashing surf outside the caves that led to the Banishing arena. "It's not just about fighting and boy stuff. There's some smarts to it too."

"Yeah, great," Charlie mumbled.

"What's wrong?"

"I looked like an idiot in there!"

"No, you didn't," Violet protested. "I wouldn't have known what to do if *I'd* gone first. Someone had to attack it so we'd know what would happen."

"I guess," Charlie said, unconvinced.

"There's the DT!" a voice shouted from some distance down the beach. Charlie and Violet turned to see Theodore bounding towards them, his face still red and puffy. The Nightmare Academy loomed just behind him. "How was Beginning Banishing?"

"Great!" Violet chirped as Charlie said, "Miserable."

"I see," Theodore replied, glancing between them. "SDOO – otherwise known as severe difference of opinion."

"Ignore Charlie," Violet said with a playful grin. "He's just grumpy he didn't get a chance to show the world that he's the greatest Banisher who ever lived."

"That's not true," Charlie shot back. "I don't have to be the greatest Banisher who ever lived – I just don't want to be the greatest loser who ever lived."

"Well, you're about to have a chance to turn things around," Theodore said, clapping him on the back. "Neophyte Nethermancy is about to start."

It was always night in the Nethermancy class.

Dark and mysterious, the classroom was located inside a hollowed-out section in the giant heart of the banyan tree, accessible only by a deliriously dodgy rope bridge that looked in terrible need of repair. Theodore and Charlie entered to find the class already full of students, all babbling excitedly. When the other kids saw them, their chatter slowed to a stop, like a car running out of petrol.

"Oh, man, they were talking about us," Charlie whispered.

"Let them talk," Theodore replied with some measure of pride. "It's not every day they get a chance to see a Double-Threat and a combat machine standing side by side."

"You really believe that about yourself, don't you?"

"Of course," he said. "If I don't, who will?"

Charlie laughed then – Theodore's self-confidence was like a kind of miracle. "Maybe you're right," he said, then glanced up at the ceiling. He was surprised to discover that it was covered in stars. Unlike the fake press-on stars from his bedroom, these looked like *real* stars. A comet traced a lonely path across the roof, flaming out before it reached the wall.

"Hologram, definitely," Theodore said, gesturing to the amazing display above them. "Probably rear projection. Excellent system. Top-notch."

"Yeah," Charlie agreed, but he wasn't so sure. The stars and planets twinkling over their heads looked so genuine, it felt almost as if you could travel to them.

Suddenly, there was a soft *pop* and a portal opened up in front of the waiting students. Tabitha stepped through and closed the portal behind her.

"Good afternoon, class," she said, nervously adjusting her jewellery. "My name is Tabitha Greenstreet, but the Headmaster insists you address me as *Professor*

Greenstreet, so I guess we'd better do as she says. This is your first day taking Neophyte Nethermancy and it's my first day teaching it, so let's just go easy on each other, OK?"

The students all nodded.

"Good," she said. "Nethermancy is the art of opening portals into and out of the Nether, and, yes, it *is* an art. Now you're all able to do it or you wouldn't be sitting here, but you can't do it on command and you can't do it with *precision*. The world is full of children who unwittingly open portals during their nightmares, but we believe that you select few have the ability to open a portal while you're awake and to open it into a particular *place*. And what allows you to do that?"

"The Gift," Alejandro Ramirez instantly shot back.

"Right," Tabitha said. "And imagination allows us access to the Gift, but what *fuels* it? What emotion do we have to tap into?"

"Fear," Charlie said, unaware that he had even opened his mouth. When he realised he had spoken out loud, he was instantly embarrassed.

"That's right, Charlie," Tabitha said. "Fear is our weapon and fear is also our enemy. We need it to do our job correctly, and yet, if we don't *control* it and *channel* it, fear will make us turn and run at the exact moment we need to use it. So, the first question we have to ask ourselves is, 'How do we access our fear?' How do we make ourselves afraid enough to open a portal when we need to? It's easy at night, during a nightmare, but how do we do it during the day, on command?"

The students were silent. Tabitha turned to Charlie. "How about you? You did it last night, rather famously, it seems. I helped you. What did I do?"

"You told me I was on the roof of a tall building."

Tabitha nodded. "That's right. Fear of heights. Go on."

"You said I fell."

"Fear of falling. What happened next?"

"Uh... I don't remember."

"I think you do," Tabitha pressed. "We're going to be sharing some very personal feelings in this class. It may be uncomfortable, but it *is* necessary. So, I ask you again... what happened next?"

Charlie continued, even though it was painful territory for him. "You said my parents could save me if they wanted to... but they didn't want to."

"That's right, Charlie. Thank you. Fear of abandonment. Keep talking."

"You said there were other kids there who could help me, but they didn't want to either."

"Fear of rejection by your peers. Very devastating. And

there was one more thing, wasn't there? As you fell towards the ground, what did I say would happen to you?"

"That I would die," Charlie said softly.

"Fear of death," Tabitha agreed, nodding. "So, fear of heights, fear of falling, fear of abandonment, fear of rejection, fear of death. One or *all* of those fears gave Charlie access to the Gift, which allowed him to open a portal."

"Not just *a* portal," Theodore exclaimed. "The hugest portal anyone's ever seen!"

"True," Tabitha replied. "But that's because Charlie's power over the Gift was raw and unfocused. In this class, we will learn to *control* it. Now, when I was trying to help Charlie open the portal, I played on a variety of common fears, hoping I would find one that would trigger his use of the Gift. You see, all fears are not equal. Very often, you must find a *personal* fear, the thing that scares you in your heart and soul, to allow you to open a portal. We will spend the next few days trying to find those fears so that you will be able to access them when necessary."

"But that's impossible," Alejandro said. "How do you just *make* yourself afraid?"

"How do actors make themselves cry?" Tabitha countered. "When the director says 'Action', how do they shed real tears? They think of something that fills them with grief, something *personal*, to trigger the emotion."

Charlie glanced around. The other students seemed unsure, nervous. Charlie knew exactly how they felt.

"I won't kid you," Tabitha continued, walking towards them. "It is a hard and difficult path you have been called to. You will have to face your deepest fears every day. Most people spend their lives trying to figure out how to *avoid* being afraid, but you will seek it out. The process may seem uncomfortable at first, even cruel, but it *is* necessary." She stopped in front of Theodore. "What makes you afraid, young man?"

"I'm not afraid of anything," Theodore said, straightening up in his chair. "I really should be a Banisher, actually, because nothing scares me. My father's a Banisher" he added with some pride.

"All right then," Tabitha said. "Let's begin with you."

Theodore sat on a chair at the head of the class. "This isn't going to work," he said, crossing his arms.

"Just relax," Tabitha told him soothingly. "I want you to meet something, a creature from the Nether."

She stepped over to a small cage that rested on a desk that had been carved from the innards of the banyan tree.

The cage was covered in a black velvet cloth. Tabitha reached her hand under the velvet and pulled something out.

"This is a Snark," she said.

Everyone leaned forwards, straining to see the thing she held in her hand. It was a tiny, fragile-looking ball of fur with large, round eyes and a small, beaklike mouth.

It cooed gently.

"Aw, it's cute!" one of the girls in the class exclaimed.

"The Snark feeds on fear the same way a mosquito feeds on blood," Tabitha continued. "As a mosquito drinks blood, its body gets full and round. The Snark, when it feeds, changes as well."

"Into what?" Theodore asked.

"You'll find out," Tabitha said, placing the Snark on his shoulder. It was as light as a feather and it clung to him on its spindly little bird legs. "Now," Tabitha said, "close your eyes."

Theodore did.

"So you're not afraid of anything?" she asked.

"Nope. Always been that way. I'm a combat machine – no emotions, raw power."

"Like your father?"

"Definitely. He's one of the toughest Banishers around.

He's on a black op right now. You know what a black op is?"

"I do," Tabitha said. The Snark chirped and cooed softly on Theodore's shoulder. "He must have been very proud to find out that you were accepted into the Nightmare Academy."

"Absolutely. Like father, like son."

"But that's not really true, is it?" Tabitha continued. "How do you think he'll feel when he finds out you're not a Banisher like he is?"

"But, see, I *am* a Banisher. There was just a problem with that stupid Trout, which I tried to explain to the Headmaster. I think it was sick or something."

"Your father didn't have any problems like that, did he?"

"I guess not," Theodore said, shifting uncomfortably. "But, the thing is, our whole lives can't be determined by some dumb, defective fi—"

"The truth is, you're not really a Banisher," said Tabitha, interrupting him as she moved in closer. "You *wanted* to be, your father *expected* you to be, but you couldn't do it. You're not strong enough, are you?"

"But I *am*," Theodore said quickly.

Something happened to the Snark. It started to swell, puffing out at odd angles. The fuzzy yellow fur dropped off, leaving only bare, raw skin. A barbed tail poked out of its flesh and a jaw began to protrude – a jaw with small, sharp fangs.

Seeing this, Tabitha pressed on, more intensely now.

"You're a disappointment to him."

"No..."

"All he wanted was a son like him, a strong young man, a *combat machine* who could follow in his footsteps and make him proud. Instead, he got you – a weak little *Nethermancer*."

Theodore was near tears now, but the Snark—

It was *much* bigger, the size of a vulture. Black bat wings exploded from its back and it hovered just behind Theodore with an eerie vibrating sound. Below its large, lidless eyes, a snakelike tongue flickered in and out of its toothy snout, as if it could almost *taste* the fear in the air.

"Maybe he won't care..." Theodore said softly, starting to rock back and forth. "Maybe he'll be proud of me anyway."

"But you don't really believe that, do you? You think he'll care very much. What if he doesn't want you to be his son? What if he can't stand to even *look* at you?"

"What if he's ashamed of me!" Theodore suddenly shouted, his eyes snapping open in panic. "*What if he doesn't love me any more?*"

With that, the Snark grew to the size of a hyena, its forked tongue greedily tasting the air like a drowning man gulping his first breath of oxygen.

"Stop it!" Charlie shouted at Tabitha. He turned to Theodore. "Don't believe her – you know it's not true."

But Theodore couldn't hear him.

His panic grew quickly, like a snowball rolling downhill. Suddenly, there was a soft *pop* and a small portal opened up in front of him, no bigger than a bicycle wheel, its rim crackling with purple flame. Through it, Charlie could see the barren plains of the Nether and a gaggle of creatures he recognised as Gremlins. Startled, they scattered away from the open portal, disappearing into the dark crevices of the rocks.

"That's good," Tabitha said, taking Theodore by the face and forcing him to focus his attention on her. "You did it."

"What?" Theodore said dazedly, as if waking from a deep sleep.

"You opened a portal into the Nether, to the first ring."

Theodore stared in amazement at the portal that shimmered in front of him. "I did that?" he asked.

Tabitha nodded and smiled warmly. "Congratulations... *Nethermancer*."

Theodore's breathing slowed and a small smile crept

across his swollen face. The portal wavered a moment, like a mirage, then disappeared with an audible *pop*.

Above him, the Snark began to shrink. Its fanged jaw folded back into its face, the tail and bat wings receded into its flesh and, as it dropped down, its fuzzy yellow hair regrew until it was, once again, an adorable little yellow ball of fluff perched delicately on Theodore's shoulder.

It chirped and cooed. The class stared in amazement.

"Wow," Alejandro muttered.

"It seems we have found your key, Theodore," Tabitha said. "The personal fear that, with practice, you can use to create portals whenever you need to. Most people think that Banishers are the tough ones, but *we* know that the scariest things are not out there... but in here." She tapped her head. "And we face those fears every day. I'm proud of you."

"Thank you, Professor Greenstreet," Theodore said quietly, and hopped off the chair.

"So... who's next?" Tabitha asked.

Not a single student raised a hand.

She smiled ruefully. "Nervous? I don't blame you. I told you our work here would seem difficult, even cruel, but it *is* necessary if you're to gain mastery of your powers. Everyone will have to take a turn. Let's start with you." She gestured to a slight young girl with mousy brown hair. Hesitantly, the girl got up and walked to the front.

It continued that way for almost two hours.

All of the students sat down in the chair and had a fresh Snark placed on their shoulders. Tabitha questioned them, gently at first, using the Snark and her own experience as a guide. She probed for their fears the same way a dentist probes a tooth to find the raw nerve.

Some students had a breakthrough and managed to create a small portal that wavered hesitantly in the air for a few seconds before disappearing. Others never got that far – their fears had not yet been fully exposed or they were not advanced enough with the Gift to make use of them. Finally, everyone had taken a turn.

Everyone but Charlie.

"I guess that just leaves me," he said.

"It does," Tabitha agreed with some reluctance.

"You don't want me to go, do you?" Charlie said with a sudden understanding. "You're afraid I'll... do something bad again."

This was true, Tabitha realised, and yet, how else could he learn?

"We're just going to start *very small*," she said reassuringly. "Step on up."

Charlie walked to the chair next to Tabitha and sat down. She reached into the cage, withdrew a Snark and placed it on his shoulder.

"Close your eyes," she said.

Charlie did. Almost unconsciously, the rest of the class drew back, shying away from him, from what he might *do*.

"Now this isn't about the size of the portal we open or how far into the Nether it goes... This is about *control*. Let's just see if we can tap into a small fear and open a gateway no further than the 1st ring."

"OK," Charlie said with a nod. The Snark nuzzled up against his neck, tickling him.

"How many people in the world have the Gift, Charlie?"

"Two per cent."

"And of those, how many are a Double-Threat?"

Charlie didn't answer right away. He could see where she was leading him, but he didn't want to follow.

"Charlie?"

"One every twenty or thirty years," he said finally. He could feel unease rising in him like a black tide. The Snark suddenly started to transform – hair dropped off quickly as its bare skin bulged and bubbled rapidly.

Tabitha was clearly shocked at how fast it was

changing. "I think we should stop for today," she said.

But Charlie couldn't hear her. "I'm a freak," he whispered, his mind racing down a track he couldn't turn away from. "And I'll always be one, even here."

"No, Charlie," Tabitha protested. "You're just different, that's all. *Special.*"

"*Special*'s just another word for *loser*!" Charlie shouted. His stomach was beginning to feel sick – sick and sour – and he found it hard to catch his breath. "I thought I'd found a home, a place where I belonged, a place full of people *just like me,* but they're not like me, not really. I'll always be alone..."

"That's not true, Charlie!" Tabitha said, glancing nervously at the Snark. It was changing at a frenzied pace now, eyes bulging, claws lengthening...

"I'll never be normal," Charlie continued, not listening to her. His panic rose like a flame fanned by hot wind.

"I'll never fit in."

Suddenly, with breathtaking speed, the Snark transformed into something monstrous.

Gigantic bat wings exploded from its back. It took flight and hovered above Charlie like a small dragon. Its barbed tail was nearly three metres in length, which was about the same size as its wingspan. Hundreds of gleaming white teeth, each the size of a railroad spike, erupted from its snout at jagged angles.

Tabitha, amazed at the sheer speed and size of the transformation, drew back. "That's enough, Charlie," she said. *"Let it go."*

But Charlie couldn't hear her. His mind spun sickeningly as he realised that the depth and power of his Gift separated him from the rest of the kids as surely as prison bars.

Even among freaks, I'm still an outcast, he thought. *I'll always be alone.*

Always alone.

Suddenly, with a deafening *crack,* a huge portal snapped open in front of Charlie, bigger even than the one he had created in the Nightmare Division.

The other students stumbled back, astonished.

"No," Tabitha gasped.

There was a sound like cannon shots, one after the other, drawing closer. Charlie dimly recognised them as the sound of Barakkas's hooves, slamming into the obsidian floor of his castle in the Nether. Finally, Barakkas himself loomed into view, sparks showering the air behind his every step.

He lifted his right arm, which was severed neatly just past the elbow, and grinned.

"Hello again, Charlie Benjamin," he said.

CHAPTER ELEVEN
A TERRIBLE HOUSEPARTY

Charlie's breath caught in his chest and he couldn't take his eyes off that horrible stump. Barakkas waved it casually in front of him.

"It doesn't hurt so much any more," he said. "In fact, I'm almost getting used to life without it. It's funny how quickly that happens." He was so close that Charlie nearly gagged from the gamey, goatish stench of his filthy hide.

"Charlie, shut down the portal. Shut it now!" Tabitha shouted, but her voice was a whisper from a faraway mountaintop.

"I didn't mean to hurt you," Charlie said to Barakkas. "It was a mistake."

"Oh, I *know*," said Barakkas, quick to reassure him. "You would never want to do that intentionally. And yet...

you *did*. You hurt me quite a lot in fact. I'll never fully recover."

"I'm sorry," Charlie said.

"Of *course* you are. Who wouldn't be sorry after doing something so horrible, unintentional or not? And yet, it's one thing to *say* you're sorry and another thing entirely to *show* it."

"How?"

"You not only took away my hand," Barakkas continued, stepping closer to the open portal. He was now only several metres away. "You took something even more precious. *My bracer.* Do you remember it?"

Charlie cast his mind back. He did, in fact, remember the large metal bracer around Barakkas's wrist, splashing dark red light around the High Council chamber.

"I *do* remember it," he said.

"I want it back," Barakkas replied simply. "That's not so much to ask, is it?"

He was so soothing as he spoke... so *reasonable*...

"But I don't have it," Charlie said. "It's still at the Nightmare Division."

"Then why don't we go together," Barakkas said, "and *get it back*." With that, the giant beast stepped through the open gateway.

Or *tried* to.

As soon as Barakkas breached the portal, he groaned in agony and thudded to the ground with the force of a building collapsing, throwing up dust, leaning precariously on the rough knuckles of his one good hand.

"What happened?" Charlie cried out, startled.

Barakkas looked around wildly. "Where is this place?" he thundered.

"We're at the Nightmare Academy," Charlie said, backing away in terror. Even racked with pain, danger still radiated from Barakkas like heat off boiling asphalt. In fact, he seemed even *more* deadly now, like a cornered animal that must kill to survive.

"What's wrong with you?" Charlie whispered, and suddenly his mind rushed back to something Mama Rose had said earlier – that the Academy was safe, a sanctuary from the creatures of the Nether.

Now he thought he understood why.

It was the Academy *itself* that had crippled Barakkas, some strange protection that was built into its branches. Is this what the Headmaster had meant when she said there were two reasons for training students here? Stimulating the imagination was the first one.

Was this the second?

"Shut it!" Tabitha yelled. She pointed to Barakkas, who

was still only halfway through the portal. "If you close it now, you'll kill him! *Do it!*"

"Me?" Charlie asked, dazed. "You want *me* to kill him?"

But before he got a chance, Barakkas summoned his remaining power and heaved himself backwards through the open gateway and into the safety of his palace in the Nether. "Treacherous woman," he growled, his strength seeming to return quickly now that he was shielded from the effects of the Academy.

He rose to his feet, towering over the humans on the other side of the portal like a temple god. "This isn't over," he said. "I may not be able to cross through *here*, but there will be another time and another place." He smiled at Charlie with a ghastly grin. "Believe me, boy, when I say I have no anger towards you – as long as you return to me what was mine. *Retrieve my bracer.*"

"I can't," Charlie said.

"You *can*," Barakkas replied. "It will yield to you. There are very few who have the power to control it. It's an ancient thing, you know – an Artefact of the Nether. I will consider your debt to me paid in full if only you'll return it to my palace. I will grant you safe passage."

"How can I believe you?" Charlie asked.

"Because I just gave you my *word*," Barakkas replied.

"Don't you agree that *I* should be the mistrustful one? After all, I'm the one who suffered grievous harm. I'm the one who will never again be whole." He rubbed his thumb over the stump. It was just beginning to heal, but as Barakkas raked his nail over the newly forming skin, black blood oozed out.

Charlie winced.

"I'm no assassin," the giant creature continued, glaring at Tabitha. "Was I the one crying out for murder? No, I'm the *reasonable* one, Charlie Benjamin. I just want to make everything *right*. So... will you kindly return to me the item that you took?"

Charlie considered.

"No," he said finally.

Barakkas stared at him and suddenly his orange eyes went red with rage. "NEVER TELL ME NO!" he thundered, and his voice was so loud that Charlie actually felt his teeth vibrate. Every muscle in Barakkas's body tensed in fury and the talons on his good left hand bit deeply into his palm, drawing blood. The colour drained from Charlie's face as he remembered what Rex had warned him about – that, on the surface, Barakkas seemed calm but that his temper was legendary.

"I'm sorry..." Charlie gasped.

And then, just as quickly as it appeared, the rage left Barakkas like a lightning storm so intense that it couldn't last more than a few moments. He took a breath and all the tension seemed to drain from his body.

"No need to apologise," Barakkas replied in his calmest voice. "Perhaps you fail to understand the *importance* of this Artefact of the Nether and the *depth* of your debt to me."

"He understands," a voice next to Charlie chimed in. "And he clearly said no." Charlie turned to see Headmaster Brazenhope standing beside him.

"Headmaster?" Charlie said.

"Hello, Charlie. Goodbye, Barakkas."

And with that, the Headmaster waved her hand and the giant portal that Charlie had created slammed closed, cutting off Barakkas's howl of rage.

"This is an ominous occurrence," the Headmaster said later that night as she, Rex, Tabitha and Pinch held council in her study. "I would not have expected the boy to return to the castle of Barakkas so quickly. If the Academy's defences had not held, it could have been a tragedy. At least we know the Guardian is still strong."

"It all happened so *fast*," Tabitha said. "I've never seen anyone tap into their core fear so quickly. And did you see the Snark?"

The Headmaster nodded. "The boy is exceedingly powerful."

"Which is why," Pinch said, "as I advocated earlier, he should be—"

"He will *not* be Reduced," Rex snapped, turning on him. "Least not while I'm around to stop it."

"We're quite beyond that now," the Headmaster said mildly. "Forces have been put into motion that we must address. Let's look at what we *know*. Barakkas wants the bracer back, which confirms what we suspected – that it is of enormous importance to him."

"He said it took great power to control it," Tabitha said. He called it 'an Artefact of the Nether'."

"Yes, there are four Artefacts," the Headmaster replied. "Each of the Named possesses one. We are unsure of their exact purpose, but anything Barakkas wants this badly, we must prevent him from *getting*."

"Why did he ask the kid to bring it to him?" Rex asked.

"Because Charlie is the only one who *can*," Tabitha answered. "Barakkas said that the bracer would yield to Charlie, and, apart from the Headmaster, Charlie is the only one strong enough to open a portal into the Inner Circle to take it to him. He's already gone there twice now. The more times you open a portal into an area, the easier it is to portal there in the future. It's extremely likely he'll do it again in a moment of stress."

"True," the Headmaster agreed. "And we must keep a close eye on Mr Benjamin because of it."

"That's crazy," Rex countered. "Why would Charlie ever intentionally take him the bracer?"

"Because," Pinch said, "even though he is incredibly powerful, he is still just a *boy*, and an insecure one at that. He was attacked and mocked by older students, he was made a fool of in your class and, through his recent disaster in Nethermancy, he has come to the realisation that no matter how hard he tries, he will *never* fit in. A boy like that is susceptible to coercion."

"Indeed," the Headmaster said, "and yet... I don't think he will turn on us. True, he feels insecure and alone – but it is our job to give him confidence, to become his *family*."

"That's if he wants one," Tabitha cautioned. "Remember, he already has a family."

The Headmaster's blue eyes suddenly went wide. She leaped to her feet. "Yes, he does," she said. "Come. We are in grave danger."

"I'm a menace," Charlie said, staring blankly at the far wall of Violet's cabin. It was plastered with prints of famous fantasy paintings. "I can't believe I opened *another* portal to the Inner Circle."

"What are you talking about?" Theodore shot back as he worked furiously to transform a Snark. It rested on his shoulder, chirping quietly. "I would give *anything* to be able to open a portal like that. I can't even transform this stupid Snark."

"I can't believe you actually stole one," Violet said.

"I didn't *steal* it," Theodore replied. "I borrowed it."

"Without asking," Violet said. "Which is what we call stealing."

"Well, how am I gonna get better if I can't practise?" Theodore moaned. "It's not as easy as it looks, believe me, in spite of what 'portal master' over there can do." He jerked his thumb at Charlie, then closed his eyes, scrunched his face into a grimace and yelled, "Get scared, Theodore! Be afraid! Be very afraid!"

The Snark cooed softly, not changing even the slightest bit.

"I'll never get this," Theodore groaned.

"Because you're trying to *force* it," Charlie said. "Do

what you did in Nethermancy class. Try to find a fear that's *real* and focus on that."

"My biggest fear right now is not being able to *find* a fear."

"Then use that," Charlie said. "Heck, I wish I had your problem. Not only did I almost let Barakkas wipe us all out but I actually had a chance to kill him and I froze."

"First of all," Theodore said, "you didn't freeze. That stinkin' thing just leaped back into the Nether before you got a chance to slice and dice him. And second, he never even came close to wiping us out. Soon as he tried to cross over, he laid there like a little puking baby... although I have no idea why."

"It's this place, I think," Charlie said. "It's poisonous to creatures from the Nether."

"If it's poisonous to them," Violet said, "why didn't it do anything to Xix or the Ectobogs?"

"They're off in the Banishing caves, away from the Academy," Charlie replied. "Whatever protects us, I don't think it reaches all the way down there."

"But it reaches *here*," Violet countered, "And Theo's Snark looks just fine." She gestured to the Snark on Theodore's shoulder. "It's from the Nether."

"First of all," Theodore said, "*never* call me Theo. And second..." He paused, thought a moment, then turned to

Charlie. "Yeah, she's right. Why isn't it doing anything to the Snark?"

Charlie shrugged. "Maybe the Snark isn't strong enough. Maybe the more powerful a creature is, the more the Academy affects them." He sighed in frustration. "There's so much I don't know, I don't even know how *much* I don't know."

"Say that again ten times fast," Theodore said with a grin.

Charlie laughed then. It felt good. He glanced up at one of the fantasy posters on the far wall. "I think that one's my favourite," he said, and pointed.

It showed a small squire sitting atop a rickety dray horse while holding a battered lance. The squire was staring up at a fearsome dragon that loomed high above, its toothy snout almost lost in a cloud of yellow smoke.

The impending battle was, clearly, hopeless.

"That's my favourite too," Violet said, walking over. "It's by Don Maitz and it's called *It Takes Courage*. That's pretty much how I felt on the day my mother died – totally outmatched by the dragons around me."

She was silent a moment. Charlie glanced at Theodore, unsure what to say. Theodore looked away uncomfortably.

"Sorry, Violet," Charlie said finally. "That must've been terrible."

"It was a long time ago," Violet said softly. "I guess

that's why I like to draw dragons so much. They're evil beasts that can attack out of nowhere but, with this" – she held up a pen – "I can control them. I make them do what *I* want them to do, not the other way around." She smiled. "I spent too much time being lonely and afraid."

"I know what you mean," Charlie said, and they shared a smile.

"Me too," Theodore added quietly.

Charlie realised that he had been wrong all along. He had thought that the *Gift* was the common bond he shared with the other kids at the Nightmare Academy, but it turned out that the Gift wasn't the thread that tied them together after all.

It was loneliness.

"Let's make a deal," Violet said finally. "We'll always help each other out, the three of us. No matter what. Then we'll never be alone."

She stuck out her hand. After a moment, Charlie clasped it.

"Deal," he said.

"Deal," Theodore added, putting his hand on top. "And, for the record, I think I could take that dragon." He gestured to the poster.

"I bet you do," Charlie said with a smile.

Suddenly, a portal opened in the room and the

Headmaster rushed through. "You need to come with us immediately," she said to Charlie. "I'm afraid something quite serious has happened. You must prepare yourself. This won't be pleasant."

From the outside, the model 3 looked untouched.

Inside, however, was a completely different story. Wallpaper hung from the walls in ripped sheets. Shattered glass covered the torn carpet, which had been bunched up to expose the plywood beneath. The refrigerator lay on its side and its contents were strewn across the kitchen. Ketchup and pickles mixed with broken eggs and anchovies in a noxious stew.

It wasn't just a crime scene; it was a war zone.

"My parents," Charlie gasped, looking around in dismay. "Where are they?"

"They have been taken," the Headmaster said simply. "You had best follow me." She led Charlie up the stairs. Rex, Tabitha and Pinch followed a couple of steps behind, causing the splintered banister to sway drunkenly. Glass crunched underfoot.

Charlie saw the message the moment he stepped into his old bedroom. Written on the soft foam of the wall were a few simple words:

RETURN THE ARTEFACT IF YOU WANT YOUR PARENTS ALIVE

The letters were large and scrawled in some dark, red liquid. Charlie was afraid it was blood.

"They are being used for blackmail," the Headmaster said, "to compel you to get the bracer from the Nightmare Division and take it to Barakkas."

"So, what do we do?" Charlie asked. "We have to do *something*."

"Course we're gonna do something," Rex said. "We're gonna find 'em and rescue 'em."

"How?" Charlie demanded. He could feel his panic rising. "What if they're killed?!"

"Control your fear," the Headmaster said. "We do not need you opening another portal to the heart of the Inner Circle. We have no protection from Barakkas here."

Charlie took a deep breath and tried to calm his nerves, but it was like trying to put the brakes on an ocean liner. "Promise me," he said. "Promise me that they'll be all right."

"I promise that we'll do *everything we can*," the Headmaster replied.

"But that's not the same thing!" Charlie said. "If you

can't promise to save them, then we have to return the bracer, like Barakkas asked!"

"Absolutely not," Pinch shot back. "It is far too dangerous. Under no circumstances will that Artefact ever leave the confines of the Nightmare Division."

"I hate to say it, but Pinch is right," Rex said. "Anything Barakkas wants that badly is way too dangerous to actually let him have."

"What does it do?" Charlie asked.

"At the very least," Pinch answered, "it allows the Named to communicate with one another, which we absolutely cannot permit – no matter what the stakes."

Charlie turned away from them then in something of a daze. Memories flooded back to him as he moved through the ruins of his house. Tacked to a wall was a Thanksgiving turkey he had drawn around his palm print when he was five years old. He could almost still *feel* the cold, slimy paint on his hand. His mother had gone to school that day to help out. In fact, she'd often gone there, just to "make sure things were OK".

But now they were not OK.

Something alien had swept through his house and taken away the people he loved the most, taken them somewhere harsh and scary, and all because he had a Gift he couldn't control.

It wasn't a gift. It was a curse, and he hated it.

On the kitchen table, he spied a large brown envelope addressed to Charlie Benjamin, care of the Nightmare Division – it was one of the preaddressed envelopes Pinch had given his parents so that they could get in touch with him. Something was inside. When Charlie emptied it, he discovered a sealed bag of home-baked chocolate chip cookies with a note that said, "We are very proud of you and love you always. Mum."

And there was something else in there as well. It was a photograph taken on a roller coaster called the Goliath. In the photo, Charlie and his dad had their hands raised high in the air, excited smiles on their faces as they waited in breathless anticipation for the coaster to make its biggest plunge.

"The Benjamin men face their fears!" his dad had written on the bottom of the photo in his quirky handwriting. After that, he had written one more thing: "I love you, son. Be safe."

Charlie started crying then. He just couldn't help it.

"Hey, kid," Rex said, walking up behind him. Charlie wiped away the tears that were hotly welling up inside. "I know this is a tough blow, but we'll see it through, I promise."

"But you can't make that promise," Charlie said. "We

don't know where they are. We don't know what might happen to them. We don't know *anything*. And it's all my fault."

"That's true," Rex agreed, to Charlie's surprise. "If you didn't have the Gift, none of this would've happened. Now we can sit here and piss and moan about how unfair life is, or we can *use* the Gift to get your folks back."

"I never want to use it again," Charlie said. "I wish I had been Reduced, like everyone wanted."

"That's good thinking," Rex replied. "Let's make you stupid and take away any chance we have at bringing your parents home safely. In fact, let's go to the Nightmare Division right now and shave off that frontal lobe. Your parents will be dead, but what'll you care? You'll be too dumb to know. That what you want?"

"You know I don't," Charlie admitted. They were silent a moment. "It's funny," he continued, staring at the shattered remains of the house where he grew up, "I was always desperate to get away from here, from my *parents*, because it felt like they were just smothering me to death. But now... I just want to be with them again."

"I know how you feel," Rex said. "My folks were the same way. They're dead now, but when they were alive, shoot, I couldn't get 'em to stop worrying about me. It 'bout drove me crazy."

"Did you love them?" Charlie asked.

"More'n anything. Sometimes, when things get tough, I think back on when I was a little kid, burning up with fever, and how blessedly cool my momma's hand felt on my forehead."

"Yeah, I know what you mean."

"My folks are gone," Rex said simply. "And where they're gone to, they can't come back from. All I got are the memories. But *your* folks... we can get 'em, Charlie. And we're gonna. You just gotta trust me."

"I do," Charlie said finally. "Is there a plan?"

"Course there's a plan!" Rex roared back. "You think I do *anything* without a carefully thought out plan?"

"You really want me to answer that?"

Rex smiled. "Look, it ain't gonna be easy," he said. "We may have to do some things that are... grim."

"I don't care."

"You haven't heard what they are yet," Rex said. "You might care then."

"I don't," Charlie replied.

Rex eyed him carefully. "I guess you don't at that. Well, here's what we're gonna do. First we go back to the Nightmare Academy... and then we head into the Nether."

"For what?"

"The Hags," Rex said. "The Hags of the Void."

CHAPTER TWELVE
THE HAGS OF
THE VOID

"How long do I need to wait?" Professor Xix asked, cleaning an eye stalk with two of his front legs.

"I'm not sure," the Headmaster replied. "Just stay here in the Banishing arena until we return, if you don't mind."

"I fail to see why the Netherstalker is involved in this operation," Pinch sniffed, walking towards them. "What does it bring that we do not?"

"*He* is not human," Rex said. "That may come in useful where we're going."

"Since when did we start depending on inhuman creatures?"

"Since we discovered *human* creatures like you are obnoxious and unreliable," Rex shot back.

"Can we just get going?" Charlie asked, desperate to search for his parents.

"The child is right," Professor Xix said. "I'm well aware of Mr Pinch's concerns about my contributions to the Nightmare Academy, and we can address them at a later date."

"They're more than concerns!" Pinch snapped. "I fail to see why we have allowed an enemy complete access to our most treasured training facility."

"Because I trust him," the Headmaster said simply, smoothing her dress. "Professor Xix has been a faithful and useful addition to our family for many years and I expect he will be for many to come."

"Plus, I think he's handsome," Tabitha added with a smile. "I've always had a thing for dark and mysterious men."

"Flattery will get you everywhere," Xix said.

"Disgusting," Pinch groaned.

"And on that happy note," the Headmaster said, "let's get started, shall we?"

She waved her hand and created a portal in the vast cavern of the Banishing arena. "Step through, please," she continued, "and be on guard. The Void is not a place to travel lightly."

They found themselves standing in what looked like a

field of tall purple reeds so high that Charlie could not see above them. The reeds were dusted with a crystalline substance that glowed in the red light of the pillar of fire surrounding the Inner Circle some distance away.

"Be very careful," the Headmaster said, stepping nimbly through the stalks on her long, sure legs. "Though they appear to be plants, they are, in fact, *hairs*, and quite delicate ones at that. If one of them breaks, it will be... unpleasant."

"What will happen?" Charlie asked, stepping forwards. His foot landed at the base of one of the thick waving hairs, snapping it at the root.

"Good going, genius," Pinch said with a sigh.

Suddenly, all the hairs in the field began vibrating wildly, clouding the air with the crystalline dust. It became so thick that Charlie couldn't see to the end of his arm.

"Close your eyes," Tabitha yelled. "And keep them closed, or you'll be blinded."

Charlie shut his eyes tightly, but already it felt like there was ground glass in them, and rubbing only made it worse. He tried to call out to the people around him to ask what to do, but the words died in his throat as the horrible dust coated his lungs, making it nearly impossible to speak or even breathe.

"Cover your nose and mouth with your shirt!" Rex shouted from somewhere off to his left. "Use it like a mask!"

Charlie did. It helped... but not much.

A horrible shrieking filled the air. It was a sound unlike any Charlie had ever heard before – a cross between cats fighting and nails slowly scratching down a blackboard.

"What is that?" Charlie finally managed to ask.

"The Hags," the Headmaster replied. "The Hags are coming."

"What do I do?" Charlie shouted, panic rising.

"Nothing," she said. "Let them take you. Don't fight them."

The shrieking was so loud now that Charlie felt like his head might explode. The air began to vibrate with the beating of what sounded like hundreds of wings. The stink of rot and vomit surrounded him and then talons gripped his shoulders so tightly that Charlie felt them pierce his skin. He was yanked roughly into the air and, within moments, he was caroming sickeningly through the sky as if on the world's most insane roller coaster, held aloft by creatures he could not see or even imagine. Finally, the talons released him. He plummeted down and slammed on to a hard stone floor.

As Charlie struggled to his feet, he was surprised to

discover that he was crying. Tears streamed from his eyes and he wondered if they were tears of fear or rage, but he soon realised they were neither – it was just his body's attempt to flush his eyes of the miserable alien dust.

Amazingly, it worked. After a moment, the world around him swam into a kind of bleary focus. He wiped the tears from his face and saw that Rex, Tabitha, Pinch and the Headmaster had landed next to him and were all doing the same. Finally, Charlie's vision cleared enough for him to see more than a few metres in front of him.

It was not a pleasant sight.

They were in the ruins of a crumbling mansion that was filled with the creatures the Headmaster had called "Hags". They were vaguely feminine-looking – at least as much as monsters with green, cracked skin, stringy purple hair and black, scaly wings on their backs could be called feminine. A crazy forest of teeth filled their wide mouths, all of them filed to razor-sharp points, and the ball gowns they wore were filthy and tattered. They stank worse than they looked, and they looked like hell.

"This," Rex said finally, "is why we don't... break... the stalks."

Charlie's rapier from Beginning Banishing class, which hung by his side, began to hum with electric blue fire as the Hags approached.

"Bring us to the Queen," the Headmaster commanded, turning to the nearest creature.

"Why should we?" the Hag rasped.

It happened so fast that it took Charlie a moment to be sure it had even happened at *all*, but there was no denying the fact that, half a second later, the Hag who spoke had been reduced to a twitching pile of meat. Black ichor pooled around it.

The Headmaster lowered the long metal rod she now held and wiped it clean on the fetid gown the dead Hag wore. The rod was covered with rune-like carvings and glowed a startling, brilliant blue – much brighter than Charlie's rapier. With a quick flick of her wrist, the rod telescoped inwards, collapsing in on itself until it was only thirty centimetres in length.

"Wow," Charlie exclaimed.

Ignoring him, the Headmaster slipped the runed metal rod back into a fold of her dress and turned to the next Hag. "Now," she said, "let's see if I have more luck with you. *Bring us to the Queen*."

The Hag swayed a moment, eyed her carefully, then suddenly turned and shuffled towards a dark hallway. The other Hags parted, opening up a path.

"Follow," the Headmaster said and began to walk.

Charlie and the others followed.

The Queen of the Hags was the most vile creature Charlie had ever laid eyes on, and yet she seemed to think she was beautiful. From the top of the crumbling grand stairway in the enormous ballroom she had taken as her personal chamber, the Hag Queen admired her extravagantly long and twisty black nails, then sniffed under her armpit, clearly enjoying the smell. The decaying gown she wore was longer and dirtier than the ones the others wore and she stood nearly a head taller than even the tallest Hag who served her.

"I hear you killed one of my ladies," she croaked as she slowly flew down the stairs towards them.

"Yeah, it was a real shame," Rex said, "but she refused to bring us to you and we couldn't stand to be separated from your beauty even a moment more."

At that, the Hag Queen laughed. Her voice was throaty and shrill and caused the few remaining crystals in the broken chandeliers that hung from the ceiling to chatter ominously.

"You're a flirt," she said finally.

"Nah, just a fella who appreciates the... exotic," Rex replied with a grin.

"Incorrigible. So, what brings you this close to death?"

"We need a Shadow," the Headmaster said, stepping forwards.

"A *Shadow*," the Hag Queen purred. "That's a very extravagant request. Who is it for?"

"The boy."

The Queen turned to Charlie and looked him up and down. Her dark eyes narrowed. "He's special, isn't he?"

"Just a boy," the Headmaster replied with a shrug.

"*Really?* That's unfortunate. If he thinks he can acquire a Shadow, he had *better* be special. Who do you seek, boy?"

"My parents," Charlie said, his voice cracking. Even from this far, he could smell the stink of her breath. It made him want to retch.

"Ah, parents. Delicious. Delicious." She licked her black lips with a shockingly long tongue. "*And who will pay?*"

"I will," Rex and Tabitha said at the same time, stepping forwards.

"You're all so *eager*," the Hag Queen said, flying slowly towards Rex on her large, leathery wings. "But I think I shall choose payment from this strong, manly specimen here. Do you have something tasty for me?"

"I'm sure I do," Rex replied, and shuddered involuntarily. Seeing this, the Queen closed her eyes and smiled, enjoying his revulsion.

"Let me think," she said. "If you want a Shadow so that the boy can find *his* parents, then in payment I want" – she opened her eyes and looked straight at Rex – "*your parents*."

She licked her black lips once again.

"What?" Charlie said, confused. "You can't have them. His parents are already dead."

The Hag Queen laughed. "The boy doesn't understand what we desire. What we *eat*."

Charlie turned to Rex. "What is she talking about?" he asked.

"They eat memories, kid," Rex said quietly. "They suck 'em from your brain and feast on 'em, and once they're done, you don't have 'em any more."

"You can't do that!" Charlie gasped. "Your memories are all you have left of your parents."

"I got pictures," Rex said. "Some letters too. Those'll help."

"But it's not the *same*. When things get tough you said you think of your mother taking care of you when you were sick by putting her cool hand on your forehead. That will be gone."

"It's OK, kid," Rex said with a gentle smile. "Nothing lasts for ever."

"No!"

Rex pushed past him and walked to the Hag Queen. "Let's just get this over with."

Giant leathery wings enfolded Rex, pulling him against the chest of the thing that meant to take his family from him. The Hag Queen stood fully half a metre taller than he did and he could feel her hard, scaly body pressed up against his back. The stink of her made his eyes water.

"Tasty," she said, and that long tongue of hers flickered out of her mouth, snakelike. She leaned down to the side of his head and licked his ear. Rex could feel his stomach heave.

"Say goodbye to Mummy and Daddy," she croaked, then clamped her rotten lips over his ear and slid her tongue inside as smoothly as hot grease going down a kitchen sink. Rex could feel it in his head, that tongue, snaking into his brain, where his memories were locked away. She drank deeply of them, starting with the most recent – the deathbed of his father.

His final words to Rex: "...my strong son."

Gone.

"Good," the Hag mumbled, and drank more deeply.

Rex toasting his parents at their fortieth anniversary party – *gone.*

The family trip to the Kern River, the one where they'd all gone rafting down the white water and Rex had teased his mother for screaming like a little girl – *gone*.

The countless Christmases and birthdays with presents and cakes and sparkly ornaments on the trees. The cheers during football games that were won and the hugs of comfort after games that were lost. The hours spent building train tracks together, laughing at films and crying when their dog Gus had to be put down.

All gone.

Even the cool hand on a hot, feverish forehead was greedily drunk by a Hag with an unquenchable thirst for the joy and pain of others. When it was done, she released him and licked her lips like a starving man who had just gorged on a full meal.

"Delicious," she said. "Tasty, tasty. All the good bits."

Rex dropped to his knees on the shattered tile of the grand ballroom and Tabitha rushed to hold him.

"Is it over?" he managed.

"It is," she said.

"What did she want from me?"

"Your parents."

He looked at her blankly. "Who?" he said.

She held him tightly then as the Hag Queen fluttered to the Headmaster on her strong wings.

"Are you satisfied?" the Headmaster asked.

"It was... quite a meal," the Queen replied, shuddering with delight. "You have earned your chance at the Shadow."

"I mean to see the boy protected," the Headmaster said. "We have paid a terrible price. If there is any trickery, I will kill every creature in here, *starting with you.*"

"I thought you all found me beautiful," the Hag Queen croaked with a sinister smile.

"You are foul," the Headmaster replied. "Now fulfil your bargain."

The Hag turned to Charlie, who was still reeling from the horror of what had just happened to Rex. "Come, boy," she said. "I will lead you to the Gorgon Maze."

"What do I do?" Charlie asked the Headmaster.

"Go with her," she replied. "At the end of the Gorgon Maze lies the Shadow. Now listen to me carefully, Mr Benjamin – do not look at any of the Gorgons. If you see them directly, you will be turned to stone."

Charlie flashed back to the unfortunate soul he'd seen wheeled through the Nightmare Division, skin hard and pale as marble. Was it possible that Charlie had first set foot in the ND only yesterday? It seemed like a lifetime ago.

"I'll be careful," he said. "But what do I do when I find the Shadow?"

"It will speak to you," the Headmaster replied. "Open your mouth and let it fill you. It will do the rest."

Charlie shuddered. *Open your mouth and let it fill you.* He couldn't think of anything he wanted to do less.

"And, Mr Benjamin," the Headmaster continued, "always remember, if things seem hopeless – *you are not alone.*"

She held his gaze steadily.

Charlie nodded. "Yes, ma'am." As he walked towards the Hag Queen, he passed by Rex, who was still being held by Tabitha.

"I'm sorry," Charlie said. "I never wanted you to give up so much."

"Give up what?" Rex asked.

It was almost too much for Charlie to bear. He walked past Rex and followed the Hag Queen into the darkness.

The Gorgon Maze glittered brilliantly. Crystals covered the walls, glowing from within. Ruby reds lay side by side with cerulean blue and dark forest greens. The colours were so intense, they were almost blinding.

"Good luck, boy," the Hag Queen said to Charlie, "although luck won't be enough. I am quite certain you will end up joining the other 'ornaments' in my Gorgon

Maze." She laughed then, the sound shrill and piercing.

Steeling his courage, Charlie asked, "Where can I find the Shadow?"

The Hag Queen smiled. "You are insolent. The Headmaster said you weren't special. She lies." She beat her giant wings then and rose into the air. "You'll find the Shadow at the end of green, boy – not that you'll get that far." With that, she flew off, leaving behind a cloud of stink.

Charlie turned to the rainbow maze and headed inside. The walls were high and slick and sheer – there was no way to see above them or even climb on top to get your bearings. He wondered what the Shadow looked like and how it could help him find his parents. Would it teleport him to where they were, or would it bring them to him? His mind raced with possibilities as he made his way through the maze – left, right, randomly choosing directions, looking always for a preponderance of green to lead the way. After all, wasn't that what the Hag Queen had said? That the Shadow lay at the end of green?

He came to a three-way intersection and looked down each path. Straight ahead seemed to glow mostly red. To the left, that gorgeous blue, shimmering like a summer sky. To the right, green – dark and mysterious, like the

Emerald City. He went right, rounded a corner and let out a scream.

Standing there was a man with an outstretched sword, hunched down, cowering, his face frozen in terror. He was made of stone – pure white marble that reflected the greenish light. When Charlie recovered from his shock, he inspected the man more closely. This was no statue, that much was certain. The detail was incredible. He could see every pore on the man's face, every hair of his beard rendered in stone with startling precision. And that expression of horror – it was ghastly to look at, so real and alive.

And yet, the man *wasn't* alive. He had been turned to stone after glancing at a Gorgon, and now he was one of the permanent "ornaments" of the Hag Queen's maze.

But how can I fight the Gorgons if I can't look at them? Charlie wondered.

Before he could figure out an answer, he began to hear hissing echoing through the maze. It was hard to tell where it was coming from. In front or behind? To the left or to the right? Or maybe from all directions. As Charlie pressed on, the hissing grew louder and more distinct, and he finally realised what was making that noise.

Snakes. Hundreds of them. Maybe *thousands.*

As his mind raced frantically, he almost tripped over

another statue – this one of a woman lying on her back, looking up at something above her in terror. That horrible hissing was even louder now and it seemed to fill Charlie's ears like a TV tuned to an empty station, its volume on high. The maze had turned purely green. Wherever the Shadow was, he knew he was getting close.

He glanced to his right and, to his shock, got his first glimpse of a Gorgon.

It was on the other side of the translucent crystal wall. He wasn't looking directly at it – and that was what saved him. The Gorgons, like the Hags, were tall, humanoid creatures, but, unlike the Hags, instead of hair, they had snakes – hundreds of them, hissing madly.

The Gorgon was followed by another.

And then another.

"Boy meat..." the Gorgons hissed as they sniffed the air. "Tender boy meat..."

They were coming towards him from all sides now, and Charlie started to panic. How could he survive this all by himself?

And then he remembered what the Headmaster had told him.

You are not alone.

Charlie closed his eyes tightly, extended his right hand and tried, for the first time on his own, to *consciously* open a portal. As the hissing of the Gorgons grew louder, he imagined the Banishing arena. It was vivid and clear in his mind's eye, and he suddenly realised that all the places he had previously portalled into or out of were shining brightly in his head – the High Council chamber, the Nethermancy room, Barakkas's palace.

He focused on the Banishing arena.

He could see the worn stone benches and smell the sweet, dusky scent of the powdery dirt. Once he had the destination in mind, he focused on the *fear*, his particular personal fear that seemed to fuel his Nethermancy ability most easily.

If I do this, he thought, *if I find the Shadow and let it do to me what it needs to, I'll be that much more of a freak.*

Though he couldn't see the Gorgons, he could hear them and, even worse, he could *smell* them. They smelled like earth and decaying leaves – like a cool, dark burrow where snakes hid from the heat of the day.

The nearness of them turned his stomach.

Brick by brick, he thought, *I'm building a wall that separates me from the other students. Eventually, I'll close myself off from them completely. I'll be untouchable. I'll be all alone.*

Alone.

That's what did it.

Like a key turning in a lock, Charlie controlled and channelled his fear to open a portal to the Banishing arena as the Gorgons drew to within an arm's length of him. Professor Xix stood there, waiting patiently on his eight giant legs.

"There you are," Xix said. "I was wondering if you were going to call on me."

"Can you help?" Charlie asked, eyes shut tight.

"Oh, I'm sure I can," Xix replied, quickly surveying the scene. "Gorgons. Excellent. I've been meaning to replenish our supply. Some ridiculous student always tries to take a peek at one during Gorgon Defence class – even though I clearly warn them – and then I end up having to cut off the Gorgon's head to bring the student back to life. It wreaks havoc on my stock. Keep your eyes closed, Charlie, until I say to open them."

"No problem," Charlie said. At that moment, he couldn't imagine *ever* opening his eyes again. Even though he couldn't see what was happening, he could *hear* it. Beneath the insane shrieking of the Gorgons, there was a sound like fishing line playing out, followed by a *thud*.

He's wrapping them in webbing, Charlie realised with dark delight.

Occasionally, stiff hairs brushed past him and he knew that they were the hairs on the legs of Xix as the large creature shuttled about, doing its business. Finally, *mercifully*, the shrieking of the Gorgons stopped.

"You can open your eyes now," Xix said.

Warily, Charlie opened his eyes. He was surrounded by writhing sacks of spider silk. The Gorgons were completely encased. There must have been twenty of them lying there.

"Quite a haul," Xix said cheerily. "Won't need to get more for some time now. It's one of the advantages of not being human – looking at them has no effect on me."

"Thank you," Charlie managed.

"Not at all," Xix said, heaving the trapped Gorgons through the portal and into the Banishing arena. "I don't smell any more of them, so you should have a clear path to the Shadow. You can close the portal now."

"OK," Charlie said. It took all of his will to strand himself in the Nether by closing the only gateway that led to safety, but Charlie gritted his teeth and, with a wave of his hand, closed the portal.

Alone once more, he continued deeper into the maze.

The green crystal walls were blazing with such intensity that they were almost painful to look at. Suddenly, to his shock, he heard his mother's voice.

"Charlie..." she said from somewhere further down the maze. "Where's my sweet boy?"

"Mum!" Charlie shouted, and pressed forwards, following the sound. Finally, he rounded a corner and saw his mother standing with her back against a dead end.

"There he is," she said. "You found me at last."

"Is it really you?" Charlie gasped. He desperately wanted to rush up to her and hug her – but it couldn't be her, could it? What would she be doing here at the very end of the Gorgon Maze?

"Of course it is," she said, and then something odd happened. She shimmered and fell away, almost as if she'd been absorbed into the column of dark smoke that now stood there writhing against the glowing emerald wall. The smoke reformed itself and now it was his father standing there.

"Hello, son," the thing that looked like his father said. "It would be so good if we could all be together again."

Charlie slowly walked up to the alien thing and reached out to touch it. His hand passed straight through and the thing that looked like his father was instantly absorbed back into the column of churning black smoke.

"Are you the Shadow?" Charlie asked.

There was no answer.

"Can you help me find my parents?"

Again, silence from the twisting, formless thing.

Open your mouth and let it fill you. It will do the rest, the Headmaster had instructed him.

Charlie opened his mouth.

Slowly, carefully, the darkness formed itself into a tube and snaked down his throat. It was cold and he could feel it spreading throughout his body, its smoky, dark tendrils filling all his crevices – his heart, his lungs, out to the tips of his fingers and down to the heels of his feet.

Finally, the coldness went away and it was as if it had never been there. But the Shadow, which just moments ago had been swirling in front of him, was now gone.

It was inside him.

Chapter Thirteen
The Shadow Knows

After a few frustrating attempts, Charlie finally managed to portal back to the Banishing arena and was happy to find Rex, Tabitha, Pinch and the Headmaster waiting for him.

"You did it!" Tabitha nearly shouted, hugging him tightly. "Are you OK?"

"Sure am. Where's Professor Xix? I want to thank him."

"Aw, he's like a kid on Christmas morning," Rex said. "Off to play with his fresh crop of Gorgons. We're not gonna see him for a while."

"Did you find the Shadow?" the Headmaster asked.

Charlie nodded.

"And did you swallow it?"

He nodded again. "It was cold."

"I hear that's true, although I've never swallowed one. They're extremely rare and quite powerful."

"What do they do exactly?" Charlie asked.

The Headmaster smiled. "Come outside and I'll show you."

The balmy tropical breeze felt good on Charlie's face after spending so much time in the Nether. He basked in it, breathing it in. It warmed him from the inside.

"You see where the sun is?" the Headmaster said, pointing. Charlie looked. The sun was low in the western sky, directly behind him. "Now look at your shadow."

Charlie looked in front of him to where he expected his shadow to be. *It wasn't there.* "Huh?" he said.

"Keep looking."

Charlie turned around, only to discover that his shadow stretched out behind him – pointing in the direction of the sun.

"But that's impossible," he said. "Your shadow can't point towards the sun; it has to point away."

"True," the Headmaster replied, "but this is not your real shadow. That is now gone. It has been replaced by *this* Shadow, and *this* Shadow will always point in the direction of the thing you love the most – in this case, your parents. It will lead us straight to them."

"Excellent!" Charlie said. "Let's get going. Let's hunt for them now, before it gets dark."

"You sure you're ready?" Tabitha asked. "You've just been through quite an ordeal."

"And my parents are going through a worse one," he replied. He had no idea exactly *what* they were suffering, but he knew it was, at best, horrible.

"Fine," the Headmaster said. "Your Shadow is pointing west. We will travel in that direction, adjusting our course as necessary based on what the Shadow tells us, until we discover their precise location." She waved her hand and opened a portal. "Let's begin."

After a quick stop in a desolate part of the Nether, the Headmaster opened another portal back to Earth and they all stepped through into a dusty ravine full of cactus and the occasional sagebrush. A decaying pyramid stood some distance from them, surrounded by ruins. Several men on horseback, wearing sombreros to ward off the searing heat, drove a herd of cattle through the crumbling buildings.

"We are in Mexico now," the Headmaster said. "Ahead are the ruins of Cholula. It was once a great city, until it was destroyed by Cortez. I thought, perhaps, we might get lucky and discover our quarry here." She glanced down at the Shadow. It still pointed west, straight into the sun.

"Looks like we didn't go far enough," Charlie said.

"Indeed," the Headmaster agreed. "Let's press on."

After another quick trip to the Nether, the Headmaster opened a portal back to Earth and they all stepped through on to a beach, where they were surrounded by thousands of people surfing in the ocean and lounging under umbrellas. High-rise hotels lined the shore. The smells of coconut oil, sunscreen and sea spray were overwhelming.

"How's it going?" Rex said to a large, shirtless man at their feet, sipping a pink drink with an umbrella in it.

"Uh, good, I guess," he replied, staring at them in amazement.

"Welcome to the Hawaiian Islands," the Headmaster exclaimed. "This is the island of Oahu, to be exact. It's far too crowded for my taste, but to each his own, I suppose. So, what does the Shadow tell us now?"

Charlie glanced down. "We still need to go even further west."

"All right then. Would you care to portal us back into the Nether?"

"Me?" Charlie asked, alarmed.

"You are a Nethermancer, are you not?"

"Yeah, but it would be a lot quicker if you did it,"

Charlie said, looking around uncomfortably at the horde of sun worshippers surrounding them.

"Of course it would," the Headmaster replied. "Which is precisely why I don't need the practice. Begin, please."

"OK," Charlie said, closing his eyes. He raised his right hand and tried to shut out the laughing and shouting of the beachgoers, but it was difficult.

"What's the kid doing?" the man at their feet asked, rolling to his side like a beached walrus.

"*Trying to concentrate,*" Tabitha whispered. "Which will be impossible if you keep asking questions. Portalling is not as easy as it looks."

"Oh," the man said. "Right."

"I don't know if I can do it," Charlie said finally. "It just feels like everyone is *staring* at me."

"They are," Tabitha whispered in his ear. "*Use* it. Harness your insecurity to access your fear."

"I was afraid you'd say something like that," Charlie replied, but he did what she suggested. He imagined thousands of pairs of eyes on him, all of them staring at the freak on the beach, all of them watching and hoping for him to fail miserably...

Ironically, it was his fear of failure that allowed him to succeed. Purple fire shimmered across him and, suddenly, a portal snapped open.

"Excellent," the Headmaster said. "You're progressing splendidly."

"Enjoy your day," Rex remarked pleasantly to the stunned man at his feet; then he and the rest of the group returned to the Nether.

"Ugh, Gremlins," the Headmaster remarked with disgust. They were surrounded by hundreds upon hundreds of the reedy little creatures, as numerous in this area of the Nether as humans had been on the beach in Oahu. "Pinch, do you have a mobile phone on you?"

"Of course," he replied. "But it won't work here."

"May I have it, please?"

Pinch handed it over. "Here you go, but, like I said, it won't get reception until we go back to—"

But before he could get out the rest of the sentence, she threw the mobile phone as far away from their little group as she could. The Gremlins swarmed all over it, desperate for its meagre electricity, fighting like sharks warring over a bit of chum.

"Hey!" Pinch shouted.

"Gremlins are like gnats," the Headmaster said, "and, like gnats, I find them very aggravating. This will free us of them at least for a moment."

"But my *phone*," Pinch muttered.

While he pouted, Tabitha turned to Charlie. "We're in the 1st ring. Why did you pick this place in the Nether?"

"I didn't really," he replied with a shrug. "I was just trying not to go too deep... to where the really bad things are."

"You're beginning to be able to control it," she said with a smile. "That's amazing in so short a time."

"Aw, it's no big deal," Charlie said, flushing with pride.

"Excuse me?" Pinch asked, stepping forwards. "Could we please get out of here before the Gremlins start investigating the rest of my electronic goodies?"

"If you insist," the Headmaster said, and with a wave of her hand, she created another portal and they stepped through.

They found themselves in China this time, knee-deep in a rice paddy. Farmers worked around them, collecting the rice, barely noticing their presence.

"Ecch," Tabitha said. "You could have warned us we were going to get wet."

"You'll dry," the Headmaster replied. "How are we looking, Mr Benjamin?"

Charlie glanced around. "The Shadow's pointing south," he said. "I guess we've gone as far west as we need to."

"Good. We're making progress then." With a wave of her hand, the Headmaster portalled them back into the Nether, then through another portal and on to a busy city street. A horn wailed loudly.

"Move!" Rex shouted, and they all leaped aside, narrowly avoiding being crushed by a bus.

"Ah, the city of Perth," the Headmaster remarked. "I've always been fond of Australia. Perhaps it's because, as a child, I always wanted a pet kangaroo. I imagined living in its pouch as it hopped from place to place, safe and secure. I would have called it Mr Snuggles."

"Too much information," Rex muttered.

"Grouch," the Headmaster teased.

"Excuse me," Charlie said, checking the Shadow, which was pointing north. "I don't mean to interrupt, but we went too far."

"Interesting," the Headmaster replied. "We're looking for a place south of China, north of Australia. Any thoughts?"

"There's nothing there," Rex said. "That's just open ocean, right?"

"Yes, unless you want to count the hundreds of

islands, as well as all of Indonesia and the Philippines," Pinch replied, voice dripping with sarcasm.

"Well, look who put on his smarty pants this morning," Rex said. "Geography was never exactly my speciality."

"And exactly what *is* your speciality?" Pinch shot back.

"Beating up Facilitators. I've always been real good at that."

"That kind of violent talk is uncalled for!" Pinch snapped, but before he could continue, Charlie stepped between them.

"Could we focus on finding my parents, please?" he said. "I'm sure they're really scared."

"Quite right," the Headmaster agreed. "We're looking for somewhere remote, probably somewhere underground, hidden from view."

"Borneo maybe," Tabitha suggested. "It's remote."

"True," the Headmaster replied, "but it lacks *drama*. Verminion has always had a flair for the dramatic."

"Krakatoa," Charlie said suddenly. Everyone turned to him. "What about Krakatoa, under the volcano? My mother taught me about it in our geography class. It's remote, hidden and definitely dramatic."

"Indeed it is," the Headmaster exclaimed. "I'm sure you're right. In fact, I'd bet my life on it."

"Well, you're about to get your chance," Rex said, and casually pointed to a large truck that was quickly bearing down on them.

The Headmaster immediately created a portal. They all jumped into it as the truck blared its horn and barrelled through the spot where they'd once stood.

Without missing a beat, the Headmaster opened another portal inside the Nether and they stepped through, to find themselves standing at the lip of the world's most famous volcano, scattering a herd of surprised mountain goats. The enormous hollow in the centre of the crater seemed to stretch below them for an eternity. Steam issued through vents in the grey volcanic rock.

"Krakatoa," the Headmaster said. "It's been many years since it last erupted, but that doesn't mean it's dormant. Where is the Shadow pointing now?"

"Straight down," Charlie said, pointing to where it arrowed beneath them towards the heart of the volcano.

"Excellent," she replied. "We have found our place. Now, because we don't know the *precise* location of your parents, I will open a series of portals, one after another, into the caverns underneath Krakatoa. Although we will use those portals to hunt for your family, we will not actually go *through* one until we see your parents on the other side."

"Then what?" Charlie asked.

"Then the fun starts," Rex said with a grin. "We fight."

"Prepare yourselves," the Headmaster warned. "We're about to begin."

They returned to the Nether, where the Headmaster opened her first portal into the caverns underneath Krakatoa. Through it, the group could see a gigantic tube the size of a train tunnel, carved from the volcanic rock. Lava flowed down a trench on the right-hand side, bathing the Nethercreatures that swarmed there in a harsh red glow. Charlie saw dozens of Silvertongues, all Class 4s and 5s, as well as scores of Netherstalkers scuttling frantically through the uncertain light.

"Oh, my God..." Tabitha said, drawing back. "There's a million of them."

"We've found the hive," Rex said. "This is Verminion's base. This is where he's been assembling his army."

One by one, the Nethercreatures came to a stop as they noticed the open portal in front of them.

"*Your parents*," the Headmaster said. "Do you see them?"

Charlie quickly scanned the hallway. "No," he said.

"Then we move on."

As the Nethercreatures rushed towards the open

portal, the Headmaster slammed it shut and almost instantly opened another one to a different area of the caverns beneath Krakatoa. "Look quickly," she said. "We must move fast now that they are alerted to our presence."

Charlie looked and found himself staring at a giant glowing lake of lava dotted with chunks of rock that floated on its surface like scabs. The lake was so vast, it dwarfed the hundreds of Nethercreatures that flew above it. They were Hags mostly, but there were other things there too – monsters Charlie had never seen before, like enormous, mosquito-like creatures with insanely long snouts, perfectly designed for piercing flesh and sucking out the juices inside.

"Whoa," Charlie said. "This place is huge."

The creatures turned and stared at the open portal... then began flying towards it.

"Mr Benjamin," the Headmaster shouted, snapping Charlie out of his stupor. *"Do you see them?"*

"Uh... no," Charlie said, looking around.

"Then we move on." She closed that portal and opened another.

This one looked out on to a gigantic cavern the size of a baseball stadium. Lava bubbled up in pools across the floor and ran down the rough walls in fiery rivulets that looked like glowing veins. They made the cavern feel like a living thing, a pulsing organ, like the actual *heart* of the volcano. The air shimmered as waves of heat blurred the Nethercreatures that scuttled and flew through its darkest recesses.

"*There,*" Rex said, pointing.

And that's when Charlie saw them. His parents were being held hostage at the far end of the enormous cavern. They hung from the ceiling, bound tightly in cocoons of Netherstalker silk that exposed only their heads. They appeared unconscious.

"Mum! Dad!" Charlie cried out. The creatures in the cavern froze in their tracks and spun towards him.

"Good work," Pinch sneered.

"Follow me!" the Headmaster shouted. "We have no time!" She leaped through the portal and the others followed.

The heat from the lava hit Charlie with the force of a sledgehammer. It instantly leeched every ounce of moisture from his skin and sapped his energy like a vampire draining blood.

"This way," Rex yelled, uncoiling his brightly glowing lasso as he sprinted across the cavern, leaping over the small pools of lava and dodging around the bigger ones. But it was the Headmaster who surprised Charlie. She had to have been at least in her fifties to have had students as old as Rex and Tabitha, yet she was astonishingly fast. She sprinted like a cheetah and bounded over lava springs with the grace of a gazelle.

As she ran, she removed from a fold in her brightly coloured dress the short runed rod she had used earlier to reduce a Hag to a pulp. With a quick snap of her wrist, the rod telescoped outwards on both ends, so it was now the length of a large staff. It blazed a startling blue – so bright it shone like a beacon, cutting cleanly through the smoky haze.

"Look out!" Pinch shouted.

Charlie turned and saw several Netherstalkers racing towards them on both sides. "They're Class 5s!" he yelled, quickly counting the number of eye stalks that waved obscenely on the tops of their heads.

Rex spun and, with an almost inhumanly smooth motion, snapped his lasso at the nearest Netherstalker. It wrapped tightly around the creature's two front legs, causing it to stumble forwards and somersault on to its back, exposing its delicate eye stalks.

"Cut 'em off!" Rex shouted to Charlie. "Use your rapier!"

Almost without thinking, Charlie drew his rapier and brought it down towards the head of the hobbled creature. He sliced its five eye stalks off with a clean strike.

The Netherstalker shrieked and regained its footing, only to stumble blindly into a pool of lava, where it began to smoke and burn.

"Good job, kid," Rex said. "Now let's kill the other million."

The Headmaster, meanwhile, was making short work of the Netherstalkers that approached on her side. She was a blur of motion, whirling and spinning her metal staff like a blade in a blender, leaving a twisted pile of Netherstalkers in her ferocious wake. Black ichor fountained in all directions as the large, bristly hairs that covered the creatures sprayed wildly into the air.

"Wow," Charlie muttered, awestruck.

"I know," Rex said. "Ridiculous, isn't she?"

"Look!" Pinch screamed, glancing around nervously at the incoming flood of Nethercreatures. "They're pouring in from everywhere!"

"*Let 'em come,*" Rex snarled.

Even though Rex *seemed* confident, Charlie was beginning to get seriously worried. They could kill some of the creatures – maybe even *many* – but certainly not all of them. Hundreds of monsters boiled towards them from all directions like a black cloud. Some flew, some scuttled and some slithered, but they all descended with astonishing speed.

"Tabitha, open a portal!" the Headmaster commanded as she split open the head of an Acidspitter. "There are too many of them. We have to retreat."

"But my parents!" Charlie shouted.

"She's right, kid," Rex shot back. "We can't help 'em if we're dead."

And that was when they heard the laugh.

Low... deep... primal – it was the laugh of something so dark and ferocious that it found the impending massacre... amusing.

Charlie turned and saw a monstrously large beast make its way into the cavern on six long, bony legs. Like most of the creatures from the Nether, this new thing was a sick perversion of a familiar animal – in this case, a crab. Its two gigantic claws opened and closed with startling *clacks*. They protruded from a bony, grey, saucer-shaped body streaked with hectic flashes of amber. It was so big, it could almost fill a full-sized swimming pool. A head like a gargoyle's snaked out of the deep recesses of its shell, its eyes red and unblinking.

"Welcome, Headmaster," the beast said with a grin and another shocking snap of its claws.

"Hello, Verminion," she replied.

Chapter Fourteen
Verminion the Deceiver

"Begone," Verminion commanded, turning to the creatures of the Nether. They quickly backed off, shying away from the lava light and folding into the darkness beyond.

"So this is where you've been hiding these last twenty years," the Headmaster said. "Cosy."

"It's tolerable, although it's not exactly the level of comfort to which I'd grown accustomed."

"Then why not return to your palace in the Nether?" the Headmaster replied with a smile. "I'd be happy to give you a ride."

"I'm sure you would," Verminion said. "Unfortunately, my work demands my presence on Earth. Did you bring Barakkas's bracer?"

The bracer.

Charlie suddenly noticed that around his neck Verminion wore a black choker covered in red carvings that were identical to the ones on Barakkas's bracer. Were they related somehow? Was this one of the other Artefacts of the Nether that Barakkas had mentioned?

"Which bracer are you referring to?" the Headmaster asked mildly.

"I see," Verminion replied with a sigh. "We're going to play *that* game. Too bad. It would have been nice to return the boy's parents to him *alive*."

"Do you really expect me to believe you would let them live if he had brought what you asked?"

"Of course."

The Headmaster smiled. "I suppose that's because you're so trustworthy. Why do you want Barakkas's bracer anyway? It can't possibly benefit you."

"I wish to hold it for him in trust."

"You're expecting him to find a way to Earth then?"

"In due time," Verminion replied casually. "He will join us when he can."

"I'd love to know how. He's isolated in the Nether and we have no intention of ever portalling him over."

"As I recall, you had no intention of ever portalling *me* over either," Verminion said. "And yet, here I am... thanks to Edward." The creature swivelled its mighty head towards Pinch, who paled considerably. "Good to see you again, Edward. You've grown."

"It's been a long time," Pinch managed. He looked as though he was going to faint.

"What?" Charlie said, stunned. "*Pinch* was the one who portalled you here?"

"Oh, yes indeed," Verminion replied, slowly scuttling towards the group on his six gigantic legs. "He was around your age, I suppose. Isn't that right, Edward?"

"Yes," Pinch agreed, backing up a couple of steps.

"He was incredibly powerful with the Gift. A 'Double-Threat', I believe he was called. Those of us in the Nether, the ones you call the 'Named', watched his growth with great interest... as we do yours, young Nethermancer."

Charlie swallowed hard.

"That's far enough, Verminion," Rex warned, uncoiling his lasso and drawing his short sword. "Don't make me turn you into a seafood salad."

"Oooh, *scary*," Verminion replied with a dismissive wave of his powerful claw – although Charlie noticed that the giant beast did, in fact, stop.

"It is true," the Headmaster conceded, "that Pinch made mistakes in his youth, and he paid a monstrous, unforgivable price."

"What happened?" Charlie asked.

"I was Reduced," Pinch said, his voice barely a whisper. "Director Dyer – he was the Director before Goodnight – called me 'an abomination, a monster that had to be tamed'."

Suddenly, it all made sense. Pinch didn't *lose* the Gift. It was *taken* from him. He had been one of the strongest – a Double-Threat, like Charlie and the Headmaster herself – but, unlike them, Pinch's Gift had been brutally yanked away from him when he was just a child.

No wonder he was angry.

How alone he must feel, Charlie thought. *How miserable he must be, surrounded by people with the Gift when he was once one of the strongest of all.*

"Oh, dear," Verminion said, his voice dripping with mock sympathy. "They made you just like the rest of the humans, didn't they, Edward? Average and feeble. My, how the mighty have fallen."

"Because you lied to me!" Pinch suddenly shouted. "I believed you when you said you would help me seek revenge against everyone who tormented me."

"Ah, a boy and his crab," Rex said. "I love that story."

"And speaking of those who tormented me," Pinch said, turning to Rex, "you were the worst of them, Rexford – ever since we were Noobs."

"Because you deserved it," Rex shot back.

"How?" Pinch asked. "What did I ever do that made you hate me so much? That made *all of you* hate me so much?"

"We never hated you," Rex replied. "We just didn't like you. There's a difference."

"Don't you dare speak for me," Tabitha said. "I was never mean to you, Edward. I always treated you nicely."

"Only because it made you feel *superior*," he snapped. "Give weird, freakish Pinch a few crumbs of kindness and he'll come begging for more, like a dog."

"Knock it off," Rex said. "You're just trying to rewrite history. You were arrogant and conceited. You never wanted anything to do with the rest of us because you thought you were *better* than we were."

"No," Pinch said quietly. "You just *assumed* I thought that because I was always alone – but that was only because there was no one else who understood what I was going through."

Tell me about it, Charlie thought.

"I felt so isolated," Pinch continued. "I never asked to be different or powerful. I only wanted to be like everyone else."

"And now you are," Verminion said smoothly.

His words were like a shot to the heart. There was a deep silence then, broken finally by Pinch.

"Yes, now I am," he said. "And I take responsibility for my part in it. I made grave mistakes. I felt so lost and alone back then that I ran away from the Nightmare Academy and portalled to the house where I grew up – and that's when it happened."

"You opened a gateway to the Inner Circle, didn't you?" Charlie said quietly.

Pinch nodded. "To Verminion's palace. It was purely by accident."

"Oh, I'm sure Charlie knows *exactly* how such a thing could happen," Verminion said with another snap of his monstrous claws.

"He talked to me," Pinch continued. "And made promises... things he would do for me if only I would bring him to Earth."

"And you *did*, didn't you?" Verminion said, his voice low and seductive. "My, how *strong* you were back then."

"What happened after he came through?" Charlie asked.

"It was a slaughter," Rex said, his voice cracking a little. "Verminion killed everyone in the house, everyone in the town, everyone... but Pinch."

"Why *didn't* you kill me?" Pinch groaned. "You killed my parents right in front of me. You should have killed me too."

"And spare you your delicious suffering?"

"Shut up, Verminion," Rex growled. "You've done enough."

"Me?" Verminion replied. "What about *you*? A bomb does not go off by itself – someone has to light the fuse. You lit it with your torment of Edward and it went off when he brought me through to your world. You bear as much responsibility for this as he does."

Rex seemed to deflate. He took a stumbling step backwards. It was the first time Charlie had seen him less then sure. "You're right," he said finally, then turned to Pinch. "I'm sorry, Edward. I really didn't know how you were suffering. I was just a kid then, like you. I thought you didn't like me, and I guess I got defensive and attacked." He looked Pinch straight in the eyes. "I was wrong and I apologise. I mean that."

"Me too," Tabitha added.

Pinch nodded. "Thank you both."

"Oh, how touching..." Verminion said. "I just may cry."

"You filthy—" Rex began, walking towards him.

"Enough!" the Headmaster shouted. "Fight a battle you can *win*, Rexford."

Rex's slate eyes held her gaze steadily. After a moment, he backed away. The Headmaster turned to Verminion. "It is true that, many years ago, Pinch allowed you to enter our world. And yet, after the initial horror of your arrival, you have been strangely silent. Are you not as great a threat as we imagined?"

"The time will come when you will see my fury unleashed."

"But that time is not now?"

"Soon," Verminion said, and crab-walked back towards Charlie's parents, who hung suspended in their cocoons above pools of bubbling lava. "Wake up, little ones," he said, tapping each of them with a giant claw.

Slowly, Olga and Barrington opened their eyes.

"Charlie?" Olga rasped, seeing him.

"It's OK, Mum. We're here to rescue you."

"No... run," his father croaked. "It's... *terrible* here."

"Don't worry," Charlie said. "We're going to take you home."

"Are you really?" Verminion asked, then reached up and wrapped a gigantic claw around each of Charlie's parents.

"What are you doing?" Charlie gasped. Without even realising it, he started to run towards Verminion.

"Stop!" the Headmaster said, blocking his path.

"But he'll kill them."

"No, he won't," she replied. "They're the only leverage he has with you, and he *needs* you because—"

Suddenly, she stopped. She was staring at Charlie's feet.

Something was wrong.

She couldn't quite put her finger on it. It had to do with the rough volcanic rock where Charlie stood. There was something odd about it – something that had to do with why Verminion needed him...

"*We have been deceived,*" she suddenly shouted.

"Say goodbye to Mummy and Daddy," Verminion chuckled, and with one quick snip of those terrible claws, *he sliced Olga and Barrington cleanly in half.*

"NOOO!" Charlie screamed as his parents' bodies tumbled into the lava below.

The Headmaster was yelling at him then, trying urgently to tell him something, but Charlie couldn't hear a single word. The sheer horror of the moment overwhelmed him. He reeled backwards, his mind spinning crazily.

Did that really just happen? Are my parents really dead?

"No..." he gasped again, and dropped to his knees.

His parents had been horribly murdered right in front of him.

He was all alone.

There were other voices around him now, Tabitha and Rex – even Pinch – seemed to be talking, but the words were lost in the tide of panic that swept over him like an ocean wave, drowning him in its icy cold depths. He drifted further and further away from them in the grip of a current too strong to swim against.

All alone... all alone for ever...

And that was when he opened the portal.

He didn't mean to, certainly didn't *try* to, but the raw horror of the moment made it all but impossible to stop. It was enormous this portal, easily dwarfing the one he had opened in the High Council chamber, nearly touching the stalactites that hung from the top of the stadium-high cavern. The portal itself was ringed with a purple fire so bright and intense that the flames looked like solar flares raging across the surface of an alien sun.

Everyone stopped yelling and stared at it, awestruck.

Then... something monstrous stepped through.

It was Barakkas.

"Welcome to Earth," Verminion said with a smile.

"It's about time," Barrakas replied as he walked towards him, his giant hooves striking showers of flame off the volcanic rock. "And I owe it all to my very dear friend, Charlie Benjamin."

He turned to Charlie with a grin.

"What have I done?" Charlie whispered.

Then the world went white.

Charlie felt something cool on his forehead.

He opened his eyes to find himself lying in a bed in the infirmary as Mama Rose dabbed his face with a chilled cloth. Oil lamps gave the room a welcoming glow. Through the round porthole windows, Charlie could see a full moon rising in the tropical night sky.

He was back in the Nightmare Academy.

"He's awake," Mama Rose said, then turned to Charlie. "Don't you scare me like that again, boy. When they brought you in, you were white as a sheet. Drink this."

She handed him a cup of hot, steaming liquid. He took a sip and gagged immediately.

"It's *terrible*," Charlie said, his voice raspy from the smoke and heat of Verminion's lair.

"I didn't ask for your *opinion* of it," Mama Rose snapped. "I'm not looking for a *review.* I just said drink it, and that's what you'll do. It'll bring colour back to your cheeks. I'll be back to check in on ya later."

With that, she shuffled her large bulk out of the door, passing by Tabitha, who offered Charlie a gentle smile.

"How do you feel?" she asked.

"OK," Charlie answered, putting down the mug. "What happened?"

"You mean after you fainted?" Rex said, grinning, as he stepped in from the shadows.

"Is that what I did?"

"Dropped like a rock. Normally, I'd consider that kinda a girlie move, but, given the circumstances, I'll give you a pass. Truth is, we didn't act any braver. Soon as Barakkas came through, the Headmaster whipped us up a portal and we grabbed you and ran like a buncha chickens. It was close, but we made it."

"Not all of us," Charlie said quietly. "My parents—"

"Are *alive*," another voice chimed in.

Charlie turned to see the Headmaster walking into the room through a portal. "That's what I was trying to tell you before you were too far gone to hear me."

"They're alive? *How?*" Charlie asked, sitting up in bed. "There was no way they could have survived what Verminion did to them."

"That would be true *if* the things he destroyed were your parents."

"But I saw—"

"What he *wanted you to see*," she said. "I believed the deception as well, until I noticed the Shadow at your feet. It was not pointing towards what you thought were your parents. Instead, it was pointing off to the right. It took me a moment to understand what that meant."

"The things Verminion murdered weren't my parents," Charlie said, with sudden realisation. "They were Mimics."

"That's right. Your real parents were being kept somewhere separate from the main chamber."

"Then they're alive!" Charlie exclaimed.

"Yes," the Headmaster said. "Unfortunately, we were unable to rescue them."

"Heck," Rex said, "we were barely able to rescue *ourselves*. It was that close." He spread his thumb and forefinger about a hair's width apart.

"But if Verminion didn't really want my parents dead, why did he pretend to kill them?"

"Because he knew that something so traumatic would cause you to panic," Tabitha said gently, "and open a portal."

Charlie was stunned. "So, it was all about getting Barrakas to Earth?"

The Headmaster nodded. "We were deceived from the beginning. It was a trap, designed to force you into a position where you couldn't help but allow him to cross over. Verminion needs Barakkas for a reason we have yet to discover, and this was the only way he could be sure to get Barakkas to Earth unharmed."

"But what about the bracer?" Charlie asked. "Do they still want it?"

"Oh, most certainly," the Headmaster replied, walking towards the bed. "And I imagine they'll do anything to retrieve it. It figures into their plan in some way we don't yet fully understand." She shook her head gravely. "I won't lie to you, Mr Benjamin. Things have gone from bad to worse. Your parents are still in grave danger and we now face a threat from both Verminion *and* Barakkas. The Nightmare Division will not look kindly upon this."

"I guess not," Charlie said.

"There is, however, a silver lining. Though they are in danger, at least your parents are still *alive*. Also, Verminion has exposed the location of his lair and we now know much more about the extent of his preparations."

"Preparations for what?"

"War," Rex said, hitching his thumbs in his belt loops. "War between the Nethercritters and the human race. Verminion's been assembling an army... and he means to attack."

"Why?"

"Because he hates us," Rex replied. "All the Named do. See, kid, they don't want to live in the Nether. They want to be here, tearing apart shopping malls, ripping up homes. Earth is a playground to them and they know they'll be the biggest kids in the sandbox. But to get here, they need us and our nightmares to do it, and they *hate us for it*."

"But if they need us, why do they want to kill us?" Charlie asked.

"Once the Nethercreatures attack," the Headmaster replied, "the terror that they cause worldwide will, in turn, cause more nightmares—"

"And more nightmares," said Charlie, realisation dawning, "will cause more portals, and then more of them can come through to attack us."

"Precisely," the Headmaster said. "We call it 'the snowball effect'."

"So what do we do?" Charlie asked softly.

"Nothing," Tabitha replied, brushing hair from his forehead. "At least not right this minute. War's not going to happen today or tomorrow. We have a little time."

"*We* do," Charlie said, "but my parents don't. We have to go back and rescue them."

"This may be difficult for you to hear," the Headmaster said gently, "but we have much to consider before we go blindly stumbling in after them again. For all we know, they may have already been moved elsewhere."

"You can't mean we're going to just *leave* them?"

"For the time being, yes."

"But we can't do that!" Charlie shouted, leaping out of bed. "What if they die in there?"

"As I said earlier, we are at *war*, and in a war, there are casualties. Now I hope very much that we are able to rescue your parents, but you must prepare yourself for the *possibility* that we may not succeed."

"We have to try!"

"We will when we *can*," the Headmaster continued, more sternly this time. "You are not the only one here who has suffered, Mr Benjamin. Others in this room have given up a great deal to give your parents a *chance*."

She nodded towards Rex.

"I never meant for him to give up so much," Charlie said softly. "I never asked for that."

"Don't worry about it, kid," Rex said. "Heck, I can't even remember what it is I don't have any more." Even though they were meant to comfort, Rex's words were like a knife to Charlie's heart.

"We will do for your parents *what* we can, *when* we can," the Headmaster continued. "For now, just rest and regain your strength. Oh, and there're a couple of people who wish to see you."

She opened the infirmary door. Theodore and Violet bounded in.

"Is he OK?" Violet asked.

"Ask him yourself," Rex replied as he, Tabitha and the Headmaster walked out, leaving the three kids alone.

"We heard all about it!" Theodore said, rushing over. "Verminion's lair! Nethercreatures *everywhere*! Outrageous! How cool is that!"

"It is *not* cool," Violet scolded. "We were worried sick."

"I'm OK," Charlie said, "but I really screwed everything up."

"Yeah, that's what everybody's saying," Theodore agreed.

Violet kicked him hard in the shins.

"Ow! I mean... that's just what *some* people are saying. Not us, of course. I'm sure it's not really your fault."

"It is," Charlie said. "It's all my fault... and I have to fix it."

"You?" Violet asked incredulously. "How can you possibly fix something this major on your own?"

"I wasn't thinking about doing it on my own," Charlie said, turning to them. "I was thinking that maybe you guys would want to help me."

Theodore and Violet glanced at each other.

"Help you with *what*?" Theodore asked.

"Getting my parents back."

"But aren't they in Verminion's lair?"

"Yeah," Charlie said, nodding. "Although, technically,

it's Verminion's and *Barakkas's* lair now."

"Let me understand," Violet said. "You want us three Noobs to head into the lair of the two most wanted creatures from the Nether and rescue your parents, something that you and the Headmaster and the professors tried *and failed* to do – and that was against only *one* of the Named?"

"Exactly," Charlie said. "Well, that is after we steal Barakkas's bracer from the Nightmare Division."

"I'm sorry," Violet said, leaning in. "Did you just say you want us to rob the Nightmare Division?"

"Well, we'd have to if we're gonna pull off what I'm thinking."

"You're mental," she snapped.

"Look," Charlie said, "I know we agreed before that we'd always watch each other's backs, and this... well, this is sort of above and beyond the call."

"You're right about that," Violet said.

"And if you don't want to do it, I *totally* understand. But if you *do* want to help... I sure could use it."

They stared at him incredulously.

"Outrageous," Theodore said finally. "Total doom, no hope of survival, guaranteed destruction." He smiled broadly. "I'm in. Definitely."

"You're *both* mental!" Violet cried out.

"Come on," Theodore taunted. "Could be fun."

"No, it will *not* be fun. It will be a ridiculous failure. There's not even a *plan*."

"Actually," Charlie said, "I do kind of have a plan."

"You *kind of* have a plan?"

"Well... yeah. I mean, I don't have every little piece of it worked out yet, of course."

Violet shook her head in disbelief. "Why not just ask the Headmaster to help you?"

"I did," Charlie said quietly. "She won't."

"Because she knows it's crazy! This is impossible. We have absolutely no idea what we're doing. We're just *students*."

"That's exactly why I need you guys. For my plan to work, Barakkas and Verminion have to believe we're acting on our own – that we're just dumb kids in over our heads."

"*But that's what we are!*" Violet yelled. "At least that's what we will be if we try to do whatever it is you want us to do. Stealing something from the Nightmare Division? Do you realise that if we're caught, we'll be Reduced for sure?"

Charlie nodded. "Yeah, that's probably true. The risks are... huge. In fact, if you asked me to help you do the exact same thing for *you*... well, I honestly don't think I'd have the guts."

He tried to find the right words to continue, something to say that would make Violet agree to join him, but he came up empty, so he just settled for the truth.

"It's like this," he said. "All my life, my folks protected me from the people who thought I was some kind of horrible weirdo – and there were a ton of them, believe me. And now my folks are the ones who need to be protected. I just... I have to do what I can, that's all. I'll understand if you don't understand."

Theodore turned to Violet. "So, you in?" he asked.

She shook her head in disbelief. "This whole thing is ridiculous. It's just... preposterous. I can't even begin to..."

"*Are you in?*" Theodore pressed.

"Oh, God, yes – I'm in!"

Charlie smiled, basking in the camaraderie of his first true friends.

"Let's get started," he said.

PART THREE
THE BELLY OF THE BEAST

CHAPTER FIFTEEN
ASSAULT ON THE NIGHTMARE DIVISION

A warm night-time breeze rustled the leaves of the giant banyan tree that held the Nightmare Academy in its mighty branches. Its gently swaying limbs allowed hints of moonlight to peek through, dimly illuminating Charlie, Violet and Theodore as they crossed the rope bridge that connected the infirmary to the broken British warship where the Facilitators slept.

"I definitely saw Brooke playing with a Gameboy yesterday," Theodore said. "How weird is that?"

"Why is that weird?" Violet replied. "Maybe she just likes video games."

Theodore made a buzzing sound. "*Ennh!* No sale. Does not compute. If Gameboys were something that chicks were into, wouldn't they be called Game*girls*?" He smiled triumphantly.

"You're seriously mentally deficient, do you realise that?" Violet shot back. "Girls like video games just as much as guys. What I don't get is why we need to steal it in the first place."

"Bait," Charlie said without elaborating any further. "Come on – and be quiet. We're almost there."

They finished crossing the bridge and arrived at the bunkhouse of the Facilitators. Charlie looked in through the small round window in the door. It was dark in there. No one stirred.

"Looks like everyone's asleep," he said. "I'll go in and see if I can find it. You guys keep watch out here."

"I'm coming in with you," Theodore whispered. "If things go bad and a fight breaks out, you'll definitely need me."

"If a fight breaks out, wouldn't he be better off with a *Banisher*?" Violet said.

"This isn't a fight against Nethercreatures," Theodore shot back. "This is human against human, *mano a mano*, and for that, he needs a lean machine of doom – i.e., me."

"No fights are gonna break out," Charlie said. "I'm just gonna sneak in, steal the thing and sneak back out. Piece of cake. Both of you stay here and keep watch."

The floorboards creaked ominously as Charlie walked through the Facilitators' bunkhouse, peeking into the cabins one by one. Finally, on the second floor, he found Brooke Brighton's cabin. He crept inside and found her sleeping in a hammock, which swayed gently in the breeze from the open windows. Even asleep, she was so pretty that he found it hard to believe she was the same person who had so recently tormented him.

He began searching through her belongings, looking for the Gameboy. It wasn't in the pockets of her trousers, which were thrown carelessly on the floor. Next, Charlie turned to the chest of drawers and opened the top drawer. It squealed as it slid down its track.

Brooke stirred in her sleep. Charlie froze.

"...Can't help it," she mumbled restlessly. "Stop or I'll fall..."

Charlie realised that she was having a nightmare. Moving more quickly now, he rifled through the top drawer of her dresser and, finding nothing, checked each of the other drawers.

Nothing there either.

"...Don't push me..." Brooke muttered, getting more agitated now. "...Nothing to grab..."

Charlie was running out of places to check in the small cabin. Where could she have hidden the thing? Then he noticed a square bulge in the pillow under her head – it was clearly outlined through the hammock below her. Charlie steadied himself, then slipped his hand into the pillowcase. Brooke twisted and turned as her nightmare grew more violent.

"...gonna hit the rocks..." she said, breathing hard now. "Help me! Don't let them!"

"Relax," Charlie whispered, trying to calm her. "You're OK. Nothing's gonna happen to you."

"No!" Brooke yelled in her sleep. "Help, I'm dying!"

It's a good thing she lost the Gift, Charlie thought. *Otherwise she would be opening a portal into the Nether right about—*

And that's when a portal snapped open inside the cabin.

Oh, no, Charlie thought. *She still has a trace of the Gift and she doesn't even know it!*

But before Charlie could shut the freshly opened portal, a creature from the Nether flew through. Charlie had seen one of them before. He didn't know its name, but it was one of the mosquito-like things that had soared above the lava lake in Verminion's lair. Luckily, this one was nowhere near as big as those – probably just a Class 1 or 2 – but its long, needle-like snout still made it a formidable threat.

Spinning in mid-air, it immediately arrowed back towards the still-open portal, seemingly desperate to return to the Nether.

It's in pain, Charlie realised, remembering how the Nightmare Academy had temporarily crippled Barakkas. This little beast wasn't crippled, however, which made Charlie think that he'd been right earlier when he'd said that the Academy affected stronger Nethercreatures more than weaker ones, but it was clearly hurting in *some* way.

Suddenly, just as quickly as the fiery-rimmed portal had appeared, it snapped shut, stranding the flying beast in the tiny cabin. It buzzed and swooped angrily, slamming into the walls on its long, veiny wings, trying frantically to find a way out.

"Quiet," Charlie hissed. Just as his hand closed around the Gameboy inside Brooke's pillowcase, the desperate flying creature dive-bombed him. With one deft move, Charlie drew his rapier and used it to parry the creature's stinger-like snout with a metallic *clang*. The creature buzzed loudly in annoyance, then flew back up to try again.

"Wh... what's going on?" Brooke asked, opening her eyes.

"You had a nightmare and this thing portalled through," Charlie answered, raising his rapier again.

The creature flapped frantically against the cabin ceiling, like a fly trapped against a windowpane, then arrowed back down. Charlie ducked and spun, striking at it from behind. The glowing blue rapier managed to clip off the tip of its right wing.

"Hey!" Brooke said, leaping from her hammock, fully awake now. "What are you doing here? You're not a Facilitator!"

"Never mind that. Just help me."

And that's when Brooke saw her Gameboy in Charlie's hand. "You thief!" she yelled. "Give it back!"

The creature dive-bombed once more and, missing Charlie, it pierced Brooke through the shoulder with its needlelike snout.

"Oww!" she shrieked as it clung to her back with its sticky fly legs and began siphoning her blood with alarming speed. She spun and crashed around the room, shouting wildly, as Theodore and Violet rushed in, followed by several Facilitators who had been awakened by the noise.

"What's going on?" Violet said.

"What does it look like?" Charlie snapped, taking another swing at the filthy thing from the Nether. "Brooke, stop moving! I can't hit it with you crashing around like that!"

"It hurts!" she wailed. "Somebody do something!"

"I'll hold her down," Theodore said, then tackled Brooke, pinning her to the ground. The creature's wings vibrated frantically against his face. "Kill it now!" he yelled.

"Let me," Violet said, pulling her dagger from her belt. But before she could strike, a glowing blue lasso lashed in from the open doorway and looped around the flying creature, killing it instantly as it was pulled taut.

Everyone turned to see Rex standing there.

"What the heck's going on?" he said.

"Um—" Charlie stammered. "We were just—"

"Stealing from me!" Brooke shouted as she prised the dead creature's snout from her shoulder. "And, for all I know, he portalled this thing in to kill me!"

"I did not!" Charlie shouted back. "You portalled it in yourself. I was trying to *help* you."

"Thief! Liar! I can't open portals any more, or are you too stupid to realise that, Noob?"

"Knock it off," Rex said. "You'd both better come with me."

"I... I can't," Charlie said, backing away.

"You *can't*?"

Charlie closed his eyes and, focusing fiercely, tried to access his core fear – the feeling of being alone in the world. This time it came to him shockingly fast. In his mind's eye, he saw all the places he had previously portalled into or out of – they hovered in front of him like glowing balls of light, some of the destinations brighter than others.

He focused on one of them. Purple flame arced across him.

"What are you doing, kid?" Rex asked with growing alarm.

"I'm sorry," Charlie said. "I really am."

A portal snapped open in front of him.

He turned to Theodore and Violet. "Let's go," he said, and ran through. After a moment's hesitation, they followed.

"Hey!" Brooke shrieked. "Come back here, thief! *Give me back my Gameboy.*" Furious, she leaped through the portal after them.

"Ah, no..." Rex said, racing for the open gateway. But by the time he got there, the portal was gone.

Charlie, Theodore, Violet and Brooke found themselves standing on the barren, rocky plains of the outer ring of the Nether.

"Give that back, you little idiot," Brooke snarled,

snatching the Gameboy from Charlie's hands. And that was when she noticed that they were surrounded by a crowd of thin, chirping creatures. "Ugh, Gremlins," she groaned, grimacing.

"Don't worry, they won't hurt you," Charlie said. "They only chew on electrical stuff."

"I *know* that, Noob, but they're still disgusting."

"I'm sure they're not crazy about you either," Charlie replied, snatching the Gameboy back. "I discovered this area before, by accident, when we were trying to find my parents." He gave the Gameboy to Violet. "Here, turn it on and round up as many Gremlins as you can. They'll be attracted to it."

"I'll do it," Theodore offered. "I can do it better than she can."

Charlie shook his head. "She's a Banisher. This is the kind of stuff she's *supposed* to do. And besides, I need you to open a portal back to the Nightmare Academy."

"The Nightmare Academy?" Theodore said. "But I thought we were going to portal to—"

"It's not for us; it's for *Brooke*," Charlie interrupted. "I'm sending her home."

"Wrong," Brooke said. "I'm not leaving."

Charlie could feel his brain starting to hurt. "Why not?"

"Because you three are obviously up to something, and I'm going to make sure you don't get away with it. Whatever you're doing, I'm going with you."

"Forget it," Charlie said.

"Just try to stop me then," Brooke replied, stepping towards him. Her very nearness was incredibly intimidating... and a little thrilling. Charlie wanted to scream, but he forced himself to calm down.

"Fine," he said, then turned to Violet. "Let's just get started."

"What are we gonna do with the Gremlins once I round them up?" she asked.

"You'll see. Go ahead; turn it on."

"This is gonna be gross," she muttered as she flipped the switch on the Gameboy. Instantly, hundreds of Gremlins swivelled their heads towards her, like rockets homing in on a target. With a groan, she ran into the thickest group of them, waving the Gameboy wildly. The Gremlins frantically scrambled towards her, leaping and jumping, trying to pry the tiny device from her fingers. There were so many of them that soon she was completely submerged in a pile of the frantic, grasping creatures.

"Why are you doing this?" Brooke demanded.

"You'll find out in just a second," Charlie said, and

then, closing his eyes, he began to concentrate on opening another portal.

The Headmaster stood before the Director of the Nightmare Division in the polished chrome and steel of the High Council chamber. She was clearly unhappy to be there, particularly since Drake was in a screaming frenzy.

"I warned you," he yelled, spittle flying from his mouth in a disgusting spray. "I told you that if you took the boy, the consequences of his actions would rest on your shoulders."

"Indeed you did," she replied.

"And now the very worst has happened. We face not only Verminion but *Barakkas* as well, not to mention an army of fully mature Nethercreatures, ready and waiting to attack."

"That's true," she agreed. "And yet... we discovered that information, as well as the exact location of their lair, *solely* through the extraordinary efforts of the boy."

"This is not a game of follow the lady, Brazenhope," Director Drake replied, "and you will not protect the boy with your sleight-of-hand wordplay. He has failed us most grievously and he *will be punished.*"

"He will not," she said simply. "I will not allow it."

"I alone am in charge here and my word is law!" Drake snapped. "The boy will be Reduced and kept under the control of the Nightmare Division until such a time as we feel he is no longer a threat."

The twelve Council members nodded their assent.

"If that's your decision," the Headmaster said mildly, "you will force me to take action I do not wish to take."

Drake leaped from his chair and stormed towards her.

"Do not threaten me, woman," he said, veins bulging on a forehead that had gone scarlet with fury. "I have tolerated you long enough because of your history of service to the Nightmare Division, but if you stand against me in opposition to all of our laws, I will declare you a traitor and use the entire resources of the ND to bring you to justice!"

"Which laws are you referring to?" she replied. "The ones we have always followed, or the new ones you seem to vomit up daily?"

Suddenly, a portal opened up in the middle of the High Council chamber. Rex rushed through, followed by Tabitha.

"What is this?" Drake thundered. "It's forbidden to portal directly into the Nightmare Division. You must portal outside and come through security first."

"Wish we could," Rex said, "but I'm afraid there's no

time for formalities." He turned to the Headmaster. "It's about Charlie," he said. "He's gone and done *something* – not sure what exactly, but I know it's not good."

The Headmaster sighed. "I was afraid of this," she said. Then *another* portal snapped open inside the High Council chamber.

"What *now*?" Drake shrieked. "Have we lost all sense of procedure? Have we simply descended into chaos?"

And that was when a Gameboy sailed through and landed with a crash on the hard stone floor.

"What in the world..." Drake muttered, bending down to look at it. Just then, hundreds of Gremlins leaped through the open portal in an uncontrollable flood. They quickly engulfed the Director, grabbing desperately for the Gameboy. "Help!" he shrieked. "I'm being attacked! Assassination attempt!"

But before anyone could respond, the Gremlins stopped fighting over the tiny device as they realised, in an almost singular rush, that they were now in an electronic sweet shop with tasty wires and cables and brightly buzzing computer terminals above and below and on all sides.

As Director Drake continued his calls for the destruction of the rampaging creatures, the Gremlins abandoned him and immediately attacked the walls and ceiling, ripping open panels to chew on the wiring beneath, scrabbling through vents to get to the juicy inner workings of the technological marvel that was the Nightmare Division.

"To arms! To arms!" Drake yelled. "The ND has been compromised! Banish them before we lose power!"

As the flood of Gremlins disappeared into the electric heart of the Nightmare Division, hundreds more poured through the portal to take their place. But they weren't alone.

Three small humans came through as well, unnoticed. *Almost* unnoticed.

The Headmaster spied Charlie, Violet and Theodore as they darted through the rampaging Gremlins and sneaked out of the High Council chamber. "Clever boy," she said and then turned to see Brooke leaping through the portal as well, just before it snapped closed.

The hallway was a frenzy of activity.

Gremlins ran amok, skittering along the ceiling and running frantically underfoot as various workers tried to repair the damage. Nethermancers and Banishers worked furiously to get rid of the troublesome creatures. The overhead lights flickered uncertainly and showers of sparks rained from EXIT signs, computer terminals and the Salivometers that locked various doors.

"What are we looking for?" Violet asked, leaping over a snake's nest of hissing cables.

"The bracer," Charlie said. "Barakkas's bracer is being kept here, and we need to find it."

"Mr Benjamin!" a voice shouted from behind them.

Charlie turned to see the Headmaster racing towards them, followed by Rex and Tabitha. Brooke trailed behind with a smug smile.

"Great," Theodore said. "She told on us."

"What do we do?" Violet asked.

"I guess we'd better talk to them," Charlie said.

"I would ask you what in the world you think you're doing," the Headmaster admonished as she arrived at the group of three kids, "but I'm afraid I can already guess. I know you want to save your parents, but stealing Barakkas's bracer to bargain for their lives is *not the way*."

"That's what *I* was trying to tell them!" Brooke chimed in.

"You must understand," the Headmaster continued, "the Named will say anything to retrieve it and then they will kill you, *all of you*... or worse."

"Exactly," Brooke said.

"Look, I'm not crazy," Charlie said. "I know this

doesn't seem like it makes sense, but I do have a plan. I'm not as stupid as you think."

"We do not think you're stupid, Mr Benjamin," the Headmaster replied. "But you are young and impulsive and may not fully understand the dangers you place yourself and your friends in, not to mention the rest of us. There is a larger picture here that must be considered."

"Yeah, but you've forgotten about the *smaller* one," Charlie shot back. "That's the one I'm looking at, and in that one, *people die.* People I know and love. I won't let that happen."

"I understand your passion, but I simply can't let you do what you're trying to do. I couldn't live with myself if I did."

"Then you're going to have to stop me," Charlie said. "Because I couldn't live with myself if I *didn't.*"

There was a momentary stand-off.

Suddenly, the overhead lights throughout the building went dark as the Gremlins continued their rampage. Emergency lights popped on, bathing everything in a frantic red glow that was interrupted only by the white brilliance of erupting sparks. Smoke and shouts filled the air.

"Look, I know I may be completely wrong here," Charlie said softly, "and I know the consequences of being wrong could be terrible. This may not seem like the most logical thing to do or the safest, but it's the *right* thing – I know it is, in my gut. Over and over, you guys asked me to trust your judgement, and I did. Now I'm asking you to do the same for me."

The Headmaster stared at him intently, almost as if trying to read his mind and figure out the truth behind his words.

A voice boomed from the far end of the hallway. It was Director Drake. "Banishers! Nethermancers!" he yelled, stomping towards them through a rat's nest of wall panels and sparking cables. "You will apprehend the traitor, Charlie Benjamin, as well as his accomplices, and bring them to the Reduction Room immediately!"

Several Banishers and Nethermancers turned to Charlie.

"Headmaster?" Charlie said.

"Go," she replied, gesturing down the hallway. "Barakkas's bracer is behind a door marked SPECIAL PROJECTS."

"You can't let him do that!" Brooke protested. "It's... it's against the rules! There will be *consequences*!"

"I certainly hope they won't be too severe," the Headmaster said, "because you're going with them."

"What?" Brooke gasped.

"What?" Charlie echoed.

"You are a Facilitator, young lady. Your job is to *facilitate,* which means to help, and that is precisely what I expect you to do."

"But the *Nightmare Division's Guide to the Nether* – Drake edition – clearly states that—"

"*I do not teach the Drake edition at the Nightmare Academy!*" the Headmaster thundered. "I teach the *Goodnight* edition and, in *that* edition, Facilitators are not mere snitches whose job it is to tattle on their team. In *that* edition, you are a valuable and critical member of a unit whose goal is to protect humanity. You started this little adventure together and I expect you to *finish* it together."

"But..." Brooke moaned.

"*Go!*" the Headmaster roared. "Both of you!"

Brooke stumbled backwards, startled, then turned and joined Violet and Theodore as they ran down the hall.

"What about the Director?" Charlie asked, eyeing Drake, who was clawing around a fallen heating duct, trying to get to him.

"Don't worry about that," the Headmaster said coolly. "We will handle him."

"Thank you," Charlie replied, and ran down the hallway to catch up to the other kids.

"You!" Drake shouted, eyes wild with fury, as he

finally arrived at Rex, Tabitha and the Headmaster. "You three will immediately assist in capturing the traitors, or I will hold all of you accountable."

"Really?" the Headmaster said. She turned to Rex. "I think you know what to do."

"Sure do," Rex replied, and, one throw of his lasso later, Director Drake found himself completely immobilised, tied up like a calf in a rodeo.

"What in the world do you think you're doing?" Drake thundered. "You know what this means, don't you? I will have you all stripped of rank and jailed indefinitely. *I will have you Reduced.*"

"Tabitha," the Headmaster said. "A portal if you don't mind."

"Any place in particular?" she asked.

"Oh, indeed," the Headmaster answered. "There's one very *specific* place I would like us all to travel to..."

Charlie strained to read the signs on the doors as they raced past, trying desperately to keep one step ahead of the Banishers and Nethermancers who pursued them.

NETHERSTALKER WEB PATTERN ANALYSIS, one of the doors said.

GORGON DE-HEADING FACILITY, said another.

"There it is!" Theodore shouted, pointing ahead of him.

"Open it," Charlie said as they reached the door marked **SPECIAL PROJECTS**. "It should be unlocked now that the power's off."

Violet and Theodore threw their weight against it and were surprised to discover that it opened easily. The four of them leaped inside and Charlie slammed the door closed just as their pursuers arrived.

"Brooke, hold it shut," Charlie said.

"I will not," she replied. "Bylaw 17 in *Nightmare Division's Guide to the Nether,* both Drake *and* Goodnight editions, plainly states—"

"I don't care what the rules say!"

"You should, because you're the one breaking them!"

"That may be true," Charlie said. "But so are *you.*"

Brooke looked startled. "What?"

"You followed us into the Nether after Rex told us not to go. You were with us when we rounded up the Gremlins. You were part of the group when we destroyed the Nightmare Division and you're here with us now in the Special Projects room."

Brooke went pale. "You *know* none of that was my fault."

"Try explaining that to Director Drake."

The door began to buckle as the Banishers slammed against it. "The Headmaster told you to help us," Charlie said. "So, please... help us."

Brooke's eyes blazed with anger. "I really hate you," she said, then leaned her shoulder against the door, absorbing the heavy blows from the other side. "Hurry up. I won't be able to hold it long."

"I'll do my best," Charlie replied, then turned around to check out the room.

There, right in front of him, was the giant severed arm of Barakkas sitting on a metal examining table. It had already begun to decompose. Skin was sloughing off in great grey sheets. The bracer, however, was still around its thick wrist, shimmering boldly in the gloom.

"That's it," Charlie said. "That's Barakkas's bracer."

"So grab it already," Theodore shouted, "and let's get outta here before we get *caught*."

"Too late," came a voice from the darkness.

Everyone turned as a tall, muscular man with a great shock of wavy black hair stepped towards them. An enormous two-handed sword was sheathed at his waist. Theodore's mouth dropped open in amazement.

"*Dad?*" he said. "I thought you were on a black op?"

"I am," his father replied, gesturing to the giant severed arm. "This is it. I've been on assignment to guard the bracer from any Nethercreatures that might try to steal it – but I never imagined that I'd be defending it against my own son." He turned to the other kids. "My name's William Dagget."

"Nice to meet you, sir," Violet said.

"Same here," Charlie echoed. "I'm... well, I'm your son's best friend, I guess. My name is Charlie."

"I know who you are," William said with a slight frown. "Didn't take you too long to get him into trouble, I see."

"That's just what he did to me!" Brooke yelled, still struggling with the door.

"It wasn't just him, Dad," Theodore said quickly. "We're all in this together. See, we're on a mission to save people."

"That's pretty amazing, considering you've been a Banisher all of – what, two days?"

A Banisher.

Theodore looked away, not sure how to respond.

"Speaking of being a Banisher," his father continued, looking him over carefully, "where's your weapon?"

"Um, well..." Theodore mumbled, "the thing of it is, there was a problem with the Trout. You know, the one in the Nether? The Trout of Truth?"

"I know it well."

"Well, it was sick or something and, get this, it said I was lying when I yelled out that I was a Banisher – crazy, huh?"

His father stared at him, eyes narrowing.

"And, uh," Theodore continued, stammering, "the Headmaster decided that, just for the time being, of course, that I should be a Nethermancer – you know, just until the problem with the Trout could get sorted out. So, Nethermancer for now... Banisher really soon. Just like you, Dad."

Theodore tried his best to smile. It broke Charlie's heart.

"You failed," his father said simply. "Don't lie to me, boy. You're no Banisher, and I was a fool to think you could be."

Theodore turned away then, ashamed and embarrassed.

"That's right," Charlie said, stepping towards the tall man. "He's not a Banisher. He's a Nethermancer – maybe one of the greatest. You should have seen him the first day in class, sir. He was one of the only ones who opened a portal. He *rocked*. You should be proud of him."

"Proud that my son is no better then a bus driver?" William replied. "Dropping people off at their stops in the Nether?"

"It's OK, Charlie," Theodore said. "Just forget about it."

"No, it's not OK," Charlie replied. "In order to open a portal, we have to tap into our deepest, darkest fear. You know what your son's was? That you would find out he wasn't a Banisher and wouldn't love him after that. *That's* the fear that let him open up his first portal."

"Well, at least it was useful for *something*," Theodore's father said.

"I'm sorry," Brooke interrupted. "But the guys trying to catch us stopped banging on the door."

"They're trying to portal in," William said. "It's SOP – standard operating procedure. You better get out of here."

"Not without the bracer," Charlie said.

"It'll kill you. Everyone who's touched it has died instantly. Died *hard*."

"It won't do that to me."

"How do you know?" William asked.

"Barakkas told me."

The tall man laughed. "And you believe that? Consider the source."

"I don't think he lied about this. He needs it, and he needs *me* to get it for him."

"You can't really think I'm going to let you just *take* it," William said. "I'll let the four of you portal away and make your escape – but you'll leave empty-handed."

"That sounds fair," Brooke said.

"I can't do that," Charlie replied.

"Look, son, there's an easy way to do this and a hard way." William drew his sword from its sheath. "Let's not do it the hard way."

Suddenly, as predicted, a portal popped open in the Special Projects room and several Banishers ran through. "Step aside," the lead Banisher snapped at William. "The children are our prisoners. We have orders to take them to the Reduction Room."

"Even me?" Brooke gasped. "But I'm a Facilitator. I don't even *have* the Gift any more."

"*Everyone*," the man replied, then turned back to William. "Your son too, I'm afraid."

William sighed deeply. "Well... they have only themselves to blame, I guess. Take them then."

The Banishers stepped forward, drawing their weapons. Suddenly, William attacked. He swung his sword with a mighty strike, which was barely parried by the startled Banisher.

"Dad!" Theodore yelled, stunned to see his father in action. "What are you doing?"

"Go on, get out of here!" William said to Theodore as he fended off a blow from a mace. "If you're so good at opening portals, open one fast!"

"I don't know if I can," Theodore replied as his father elbowed a Banisher in the throat and used the hilt of his sword to open a gash on the forehead of another.

"You can do it, Theodore," Charlie said. "I know you can." Then, as Violet drew her dagger and joined William in his effort to buy them more time, Charlie turned towards the giant bracer, which was still on the decomposing wrist of Barakkas.

Everyone who's touched it has died instantly, William had said. *Died hard*.

As Charlie neared it, the bracer throbbed with red light. He could see the image of Barakkas engraved on its side, and now he recognised the carving next to it as well.

Verminion.

Steeling his courage, Charlie reached out and touched the warm metal. Instantly, it yielded to him, just as Barakkas had said it would. The bracer quickly shrank in size, cutting through the decaying flesh of the thick wrist, snapping the solid bones inside like pretzels. Soon, it had shrunk enough that Charlie could have easily fastened it around his own wrist.

He stared at it closely.

It pulsed and throbbed, throwing its sickly red light across his face.

"What are you doing?" Violet yelled, seeing Charlie just standing there.

"Thinking about something the Headmaster said," Charlie replied. "That my parents may have already been moved."

"There's nothing we can do about that now," she shouted, stomping on the foot of a Banisher who had got too close.

"Well, there is *one* thing," Charlie said. "The bracer – it's supposed to be a communication device."

"So?"

"So," Charlie said, "I may be able to use it to see what Verminion has done with them."

"What?" Violet gasped. "You're not actually going to put it—"

But before she could finish, Charlie unclasped the bracer and, to Violet's horror, clicked the Artefact of the Nether around his wrist.

CHAPTER SIXTEEN
THE BRACER OF BARAKKAS

As soon as Charlie snapped on the bracer, his head filled with a roar like a waterfall and the world twisted and lurched sickeningly. When it righted itself, he could see four fiery balls suspended against a velvety blackness. Like portals, he could see through them to something beyond, but, unlike portals, these weren't stationary – each one seemed to move through a different environment.

Through one, he could see the inside of a crystalline palace in the Nether. It was a place he didn't recognise, filled with ghostly, sightless creatures that drifted slowly through the foggy air.

Through another, he saw an ancient graveyard of old ruined boats, jumbled together somewhere near the churning red pillar of the Inner Circle. It was as still and deserted as the dark side of the moon.

Through the third one, he saw the Special Projects room in the Nightmare Division, the very room he was currently standing in. William and Violet were fighting off Banishers as Theodore struggled to make a portal.

Finally, through the last one, he was surprised to see the face of Barakkas staring directly back at him.

With a shock, Charlie realised that he was looking through the eyes of everyone who wore one of the Artefacts of the Nether, including himself. Without even consciously trying to do it, he moved towards the gateway that looked out on to the face of Barakkas, and soon he found himself actually going *through* the gateway until it completely filled his vision. Now he could hear what Barakkas was saying.

"An assault force a hundred strong would be sufficient to retrieve my bracer from the Nightmare Division," the beast growled as Nethercreatures assembled behind him in the giant cavern under Krakatoa.

"*More* than sufficient," Charlie heard Verminion reply, and he realised that *he* was now Verminion, or at least looking through Verminion's eyes. "In fact, you could probably get it back yourself."

"Of course I could," Barakkas sighed. "But this isn't about stolen property. I'm going to deliver a crippling blow to the heart of the enemy."

Verminion quickly moved towards Barakkas, and Charlie was struck by a wave of dizziness from the sudden change of perspective. "When were you planning to inform me of this?" Verminion demanded.

"I just did."

"I have been here twenty years, carefully assembling the army that you so casually plan to use without even *consulting* me."

"I don't need your permission," Barakkas growled. "You're only one of the Four, just like me. We don't answer to one another."

"But it will take all of us to summon the *Fifth*," Verminion replied.

"Which is why I need my bracer!"

"And you will get it!" Verminion countered angrily. "I have gone to great lengths to bring you to Earth, and I will see to it that we bring the rest of the Four over as well, but do not presume to take action without my consent."

"Don't test me," Barakkas thundered, eyes blazing, "or this partnership will end *poorly*."

There was no answer from Verminion. Barakkas suddenly looked concerned. "What's wrong?" he asked.

"*Someone is watching*," Verminion replied.

Charlie quickly took the bracer off his wrist.

The world lurched crazily and Charlie finally found himself looking once again through his own eyes. His mind reeled from everything he had heard. There had been talk of something called "the Four". He assumed that Verminion and Barakkas were the first two, but who were the remaining two? And who was this *Fifth* they hoped to summon once they were all together on Earth, using the Artefacts of the Nether?

As Charlie tried to piece things together, the Banishers were threatening to overwhelm William and Violet.

"How's that portal coming?" she yelled to Theodore.

"Working on it," he replied.

Theodore's mind raced frantically as he searched for a fear that he could use. His father *had* been furious that he had failed to become a Banisher, and yet the world hadn't ended as a result, had it? On the contrary, his father had actually put his life on the line to protect him from the very Banishers he had hoped his son would one day become. And it was *that* thought that turned in Theodore's stomach like a hot knife. Not only had he let his father down; he had forced the man to turn against his own employer, the Nightmare Division. His father would certainly be severely punished for his actions, maybe even

Reduced himself, and it was all Theodore's fault, wasn't it?

How could his father love him after such a failure?

How could he even stand to be in the same *room* with him?

Fear welled up inside Theodore like a tidal wave and, as it crested, a portal snapped open in front of him.

"Good job," Violet yelled, then turned to Charlie. "*Let's go.*"

"Right," Charlie said as if coming out of a dream. He leaped through the open gateway along with Violet.

Theodore turned to his father. "I'm so sorry, Dad," he said. "For everything."

"Just go," his father shouted, leaping over an axe swipe and responding with a flurry of slashes from his own sword. "*Go now.*"

Theodore jumped through the portal, passing Brooke, who was watching from a dark corner. Suddenly, Gremlins burst through a ceiling panel and rained down on top of her, clawing at her hair and scratching her face. "Wait for me," she screamed, and leaped through the portal as well, just before it snapped shut.

The four of them stood breathless on the outer ring of the Nether.

"What was *wrong* with you in there?" Violet demanded, turning to Charlie. "Why did you put on the bracer?"

"I told you," Charlie said. "I wanted to see where Verminion and Barakkas were. I was afraid they might have taken my parents somewhere else, and I'm not skilled enough to portal all over the place looking for them."

"Did they?" she asked.

"I don't think so," he said. "They were still in the lair."

"You still shouldn't have done it," she scolded. "It was too big a risk." She turned to Theodore. "Nice job with that portal, by the way. You're turning into a real pro."

"Yeah," Theodore said, still shaken. "It was... hard."

"You OK?" Charlie asked, eyeing his friend closely. He knew all too well the emotional toll opening a portal could take.

"I'm fine," Theodore answered. "It's just... I don't know what'll happen to my dad after this. I don't know what Drake will *do* to him."

"Maybe nothing," Charlie replied. "The Headmaster said she would take care of the Director. If they're doing what I *think* they're doing, your dad will be fine."

"What do you *think* they're doing?" Violet asked.

Charlie smiled grimly. "Helping him forget he ever knew us."

The Queen of the Hags licked her black lips with a long, snakelike tongue.

"This is treason," Director Drake yelled, still bound by Rex's lasso. "You can't subject me to this."

"Calm down, pal," Rex said. "It'll all be over soon. Trust me, you won't remember a thing."

"And what do you want in payment for this... delicious gift?" The Hag Queen asked the Headmaster.

"A trade," the Headmaster said simply. "You take something from the Director... and then you return to Rexford what you took from him."

"His parents were so delicious, I hate to part with them," the Hag replied. "What are you offering from the Director to replace that memory?"

"Something even more delicious," the Headmaster said, walking up to her. "All the memories that have to do with Charlie Benjamin and his friends."

"No!" the Director roared. "You can't take that from me. I need those memories to be able to prosecute him, to remove him as the vicious threat that he is!"

"I *know*," the Headmaster said with a smile, then turned to the Hag. "You can see how strongly he feels – all his insecurity, his hate, his fear. Imagine what it will taste like. *Imagine how it will fill you..."*

Without even realising it, the Queen of the Hags had begun to drool.

"Done," she said, and with startling swiftness, she enfolded Drake in her strong, leathery wings and plunged her tongue into his ear, sucking deeply.

In the heart of Krakatoa, the lair of the Nethercreatures was a fury of activity. Hags polished the wide expanse of Verminion's shell, buffing the translucent underside to a bright, pearly sheen. Class-5 Acidspitters cleaned Barakkas's hooves by vomiting their burning juices across them while Netherbats soared through the smoky haze of the cavern ceiling high above, slaloming through stalactites.

"You're sure it was the boy looking through your eyes?" Barakkas asked Verminion, angrily flicking away an Acidspitter that had missed his hoof and sprayed his ankle instead.

Verminion nodded, absently stroking the black choker around his neck with a giant claw. "Who else is strong enough to wear one of the Artefacts of the Nether?"

Suddenly, a portal opened up at the far side of the cavern. The two Named turned as Charlie, Violet,

Theodore and Brooke stepped through.

"Oh, my God..." Theodore whispered, taking his first look at the epic, lava-filled lair. It was packed with Nethercreatures more fierce then any he had ever seen or even imagined.

"This was a mistake," Violet said, backing up.

"Yeah. Get us out of here," Brooke gasped.

"Just stick with the plan," Charlie said. He stepped forward towards the enormous monsters on the other side of the cavern. "Hello!" he yelled. "It's me. Charlie Benjamin. I brought friends."

"Charlie Benjamin," Barakkas said pleasantly, walking towards him, absentmindedly crushing a Netherstalker that failed to scuttle away quickly enough. "What a delightful surprise."

"I came to make a trade."

"Oooh, intriguing," Barakkas replied. "Do tell."

"My parents... for *this*."

Charlie held the bracer in the air. It glowed brilliantly in the gloom of the cavern. The choker around Verminion's neck did the same, responding to the presence of one of the other Artefacts of the Nether. Clearly, they affected each other in some way – the two together blazed more strongly than either had ever shone separately.

Barakkas eyed the bracer hungrily. "How did you get it?" he asked.

"Gremlins," Charlie replied. "We portalled hundreds into the Nightmare Division. They knocked out the power and my friends and I stole it in the chaos."

"Incredible," Verminion said, turning to Barakkas with a sneer. "The boy did it with mere Gremlins. And *you* wanted to take an army."

Barakkas fumed silently.

Charlie glanced down at his Shadow and saw that it was pointing to the right, towards a tunnel that snaked out of the giant cavern.

"I want you to take my friends down there," Charlie said, gesturing towards the tunnel, "so they can see if my parents are all right."

"You know where we're holding them?" Verminion asked.

"I have a Shadow," Charlie replied.

Barakkas and Verminion shared a look. "Clever," Barakkas said, then turned towards a Netherstalker. "Take them," he commanded, "and make sure they remain *safe.*"

The Netherstalker bowed, then scuttled towards Theodore and Violet. "Come," it hissed.

Theodore turned to Charlie. "You good with this?"

Charlie nodded. "It'll be OK. Just stick to the plan."

Nervously, Theodore and Violet walked towards the dark tunnel with the creature. After taking only a couple of steps, Violet ran back to Charlie, hugging him tightly.

"You be careful," she said.

"You too."

"What should *I* do?" Brooke asked, cowering behind Charlie as Theodore and Violet left with the Netherstalker.

"Just keep quiet and stay out of the way," Charlie replied, then turned to the two Named. "Once my friends have portalled out with my parents, I'll give you the bracer."

"Oh, I'm not sure if we can allow *that*," Barakkas countered. "How can we be sure you won't portal out yourself, taking it with you once your parents are safe?"

"Because I'm not leaving," Charlie replied. "In fact, I'm *never* leaving."

"What?" Brooke said, shocked.

Ignoring her, Charlie strode towards Barakkas and Verminion, his confidence rising.

"I want to join you," he continued. "I can't go back to where I was. After I let *you* come through" – he nodded to Barakkas – "the Director decided I was better off dead. Or Reduced." He shrugged. "Same thing."

"So you stole the bracer," Barakkas said, "in the hopes

that such a kingly gift would make us look favourably upon you and ask you to join us?"

"Yes, and also to prove my loyalty to you. I can never go back to the Nightmare Division after what I did to them."

"You little toad, you lied to me!" Brooke yelled. "To all of us! You were planning to betray us all along!"

Charlie shrugged. "Don't blame me. You fell for it." He turned back to the Named. "So what's it gonna be? Can I join you?"

Verminion considered. "No... it doesn't make sense. You are aware of what I did to Edward Pinch all those years ago when he allowed me to cross over. He made a deal with me and I, regrettably, broke it. Why would you come to us now, hoping we would treat you any differently?"

"Because you need me," Charlie said, walking between them. He was dwarfed by them, a fawn making its way between two giant oaks. "I mean, how else could you bring the remaining two Named to Earth so the four of you could summon the Fifth?"

"How do you know about that?" Barakkas asked. Suddenly, realisation dawned. "You put the bracer on, didn't you?"

"I did," Charlie confessed, "but only for a second.

Even though I spied on your plan, the fact is, *you need me to make it happen.*"

Charlie stopped and stood directly between them now, utterly exposed but appearing completely confident.

"You would do that?" Barakkas asked. "Set yourself against your own race? Become a traitor?"

"They all hate me anyway," Charlie said quietly.

"That's right!" Brooke shouted.

"See? I'm just a freak to them, even to the other kids who have the Gift. They're all afraid of me now." He looked up at the two monsters on either side of him and stared defiantly. "I want to give them a *reason.*"

The bracer shone brilliantly this close to its mate. Barakkas was entranced by it, by the delicious *nearness* of it...

"Let my parents go," Charlie said. "And I'll stay."

In the small, dirty alcove where Charlie's parents were being held, Violet used her dagger to slice through the tough Netherstalker silk that bound them. It was like slicing through thick rope.

"How's it coming?" Theodore asked nervously.

"It's coming," she replied, finally managing to cut through most of the first cocoon. "Here, help me. Pull."

She and Theodore got on either side of the cocoon and pulled, ripping it in two, exposing Charlie's mother, Olga. She was thin and weak and limp, like a balloon that had lost its air. Her eyelids fluttered open and she licked her dry lips.

"Where am I?" she asked, her voice raspy.

"You're safe," Violet said. "We're here to rescue you. Charlie is close by."

"Charlie?" Olga asked, her eyes widening. "Is my boy here? Is he OK?"

"Sure is," Theodore replied. "I should know. I'm his best friend." He glanced at Violet. "Well, I guess we both are."

"That's good," Olga replied with a dreamy little smile. "He needs friends. He never had many, you know."

"Just rest," Violet said, and began cutting open the cocoon that encased Charlie's father. "We'll get you out of here in just a minute."

Back in the colossal cavern, the two Named talked privately.

"The boy is lying," Verminion said.

"Just because *you* are deceitful doesn't mean everyone else is," Barakkas countered. "He is just a boy – an angry, distrustful little boy, just like the one who portalled you through all those years ago. Imagine how useful he could be in helping us bring over the remaining two."

"But he *won't*," Verminion replied. "He means to hurt us. I don't know how exactly, but I can *smell* it on him."

"He brought the bracer," Barakkas protested. "That shows his true intentions."

"You are blind in your desire for that Artefact of the Nether!" Verminion snapped. "You would let your devotion to its return cloud your judgement!"

"That doesn't make me *wrong*," Barakkas said. "If you think the boy is lying about his desire to join us, prove it."

"I will," Verminion snapped, and with a startling *clack* of his claws, he called for his servants.

While Verminion put his plan into action, Charlie whispered to Brooke. "Don't worry, I'm not betraying you," he said. "I just need them to think I want to join them, so they'll let Theodore portal my parents out safely. After they're gone, I'll portal us away."

"I wonder which one is the lie," Brooke replied. "What you're telling them or what you're telling me?"

"Just trust me," Charlie said. "Please."

Suddenly, a Netherstalker approached them, holding something in its forelegs. The thing twisted and wriggled. Charlie strained to see what it was, until his view was obscured by the gruesome, gargoyle-like face of Verminion. The giant beast smelled like rotten fish that had been left out too long on a hot day.

"My partner and I are having a... disagreement over your true intentions," he said. Charlie found the stink of his breath nearly unbearable. "He believes you. I do not. If you are telling the truth, then we will let your friends and your parents go and embrace you as a true partner. But if you are lying, we will slaughter all of you. Slowly. *With pain.*"

"How can I prove my loyalty to you?" Charlie asked.

"With this," Verminion said, and gestured to the Netherstalker, which quickly handed Charlie the small, wriggling thing it held tightly in its forelegs.

It was a Snark.

Small and soft and cute, it seemed impossibly out of place in this dark, cruel pit. It purred and cooed in Charlie's hands.

"The Snark will tell us whether or not you are afraid – and your *fear* will tell us whether or not you are lying. If you're telling the truth, you have nothing to fear. You can stand there with confidence, knowing the Snark can't possibly betray you, because you have nothing to hide. But if you are *lying*," Verminion said, his claws clacking uncontrollably now, "your *fear* will grow because you

know the Snark will expose you with its transformation...
and, when it does, you and your friends and your parents
will pay the ultimate price."

Charlie's heart began to race. He thought he had done
an extraordinarily good job of making a case for wanting
to join them. It had gone just as he had rehearsed it, and
yet...

And yet one of them didn't believe him.

That hadn't been part of the plan.

The fear that had always been lurking in the back of his
mind began to grow, and as it did, the Snark started to
transform. Charlie watched in horror as it quickly
doubled in size, shedding its soft, fluffy hair as its beak
was replaced by a fanged snout. A spiky tail slithered out
of its back. The more it changed, the more fearful Charlie
became that his hidden intentions, his *true plans*, were
going to be exposed, and that fear only increased the
speed of the Snark's transformation.

It was a vicious cycle.

Verminion smiled, vindicated. "It seems you have
been exposed," he said.

"No," Charlie replied, backing away. "I'm not afraid of
being caught; I'm afraid of *you*. Face it, you're a pretty
scary guy. That's the fear that transformed the Snark."

Barakkas stepped forward. "That is *possible*, Verminion.

Don't be so quick to destroy such a potentially useful boy."

"If he is right and I am wrong, then he must prove his loyalty to us beyond any doubt," Verminion replied, and snatched Brooke up in a massive claw. He turned to Charlie. "Give me the word, boy, and I will cut her in half. After all, if you join us, she will be only the first of many humans you will help destroy."

"No..." Brooke moaned. "Charlie?"

Charlie's mouth went as dry as cotton. He couldn't speak.

"Charlie?" she repeated, her voice now a whisper.

"Make your decision," Verminion said, leaning down to within thirty centimetres of Charlie's face. "What will it be?"

Charlie closed his eyes. "Let her go," he finally said.

Verminion grinned. "Just as I thought. The boy was playing us all along. You're a fool, Barakkas. You always have been."

Barakkas grimaced as Verminion laughed – long and loud – and Charlie could feel the hot, fetid stink of the creature's breath on his face.

"If he's a fool, then so are you," Charlie said, and he threw the bracer down Verminion's wide-open throat.

There was a moment of stunned silence as Barakkas watched the glow of one of the four Artefacts of the

Nether travel down Verminion's gullet until it finally lodged deep inside his innards, lighting up the translucent shell from within.

"What... what have you done?" Barakkas gasped.

"You want your bracer so much," Charlie replied, "*go and get it!*" He turned to the tunnel that led to the alcove where his parents were being held and shouted, "TAKE THEM! PORTAL OUT NOW!"

Violet had just finished cutting Charlie's father out of the Netherstalker cocoon when Charlie's shouts echoed down the hallway.

"What's happening?" Olga asked.

"Something's gone wrong," Theodore said. "We have to go."

He started trying to open a portal as two Netherstalkers raced down the hallway and scuttled into the alcove, jaws snapping, webbing spinnerets raised.

"What about Charlie?" Barrington asked, his voice scratchy from disuse. "I heard my boy..."

"He'll have to take care of himself," Violet said, raising her dagger. "We have our own problems." She turned to Theodore. "I'll keep them off you as long as I can, but get that portal opened fast."

"I'm trying!" he replied. "But it doesn't help when you yell at me."

"All right," she said, slashing at the nearest creature. "Dear Theodore, would you mind, *pretty please*, opening a portal when you get the chance?"

"Absolutely," he said. "Much better."

Back in the cavern, Barakkas turned to Verminion, eyes wild with anger. "Give me what's mine," he said.

"Are you insane?" Verminion shot back. "It's *inside* me, you idiot. How am I supposed to get it out?"

"I'll show you," Barakkas growled, and advanced on Verminion, his one giant fist raised menacingly, his hooves spraying fire behind him as they sparked off the volcanic rock.

"Stop it!" Verminion yelled. "This is what the boy wants, for us to turn us on each other."

"The boy will get everything he deserves," Barakkas replied, "but you've always coveted my power and I will not let you diminish it. I will have my bracer *now*."

"No."

Barakkas's orange eyes suddenly glowed red with rage. "NEVER TELL ME NO!" he roared, and leaped at Verminion, landing only metres from him with the force of an earthquake. Flame exploded around them as his hooves slammed into the rock. He brought his one good fist down on the back of Verminion's shell, cracking it open to expose the pink meat inside.

Brooke fell to the ground and scrambled away as Verminion wailed in pain before retaliating with a vicious attack to Barakkas's left thigh, tearing open flesh in a spray of black blood. Both creatures howled and continued fighting as Charlie grabbed Brooke. "Come on," he said, and turned to the tunnel that led to his parents.

It was blocked. Nethercreatures swarmed into the heart of the lair from all sides while their masters warred in the background.

"What do we do now?" Brooke whispered.

"Now... we fight," Charlie said, drawing his rapier. It glowed a brilliant blue. "Get behind me."

She scrambled behind Charlie then as hundreds of screaming, shrieking monsters raced towards them.

In the alcove, Violet was amazed to discover that she truly did have the skills of a born Banisher. She spun and slashed and parried the Netherstalkers' attacks with amazing agility, drawing from a well of power she didn't even know she had. As good as she was, however, she was no match for the endless flood of creatures that were scuttling down the gloom of the tunnel towards them.

"We have maybe five more seconds," she whispered harshly to Theodore. "Then it's too late."

The pressure was unbearable, and Theodore was crushed with the sudden realisation that he wasn't up to the task. He had failed everyone – his father, his friends and even Charlie, abandoned in a cavern not thirty steps away, clearly outmatched by two of the most fearsome creatures the Nether had ever produced. Theodore had promised to protect him, his best friend, but he *hadn't* protected him, and Charlie would pay for it with his life, pay for it without ever seeing the parents he had struggled so hard to rescue. As Theodore imagined Charlie's horrible death and his own helplessness to prevent it, the fear of that failure welled up inside him with the force of a tsunami. It was a living thing, that fear, and it grew with startling speed.

Suddenly, Theodore opened a portal.

"Thank God," Violet gasped as the monsters of the Nether overwhelmed them. With no time left to spare, she grabbed Charlie's parents and leaped through.

"Come on!" she yelled back at Theodore.

"Sorry, buddy," Theodore whispered, thinking of the

friend he was about to abandon. "Good luck." Then he jumped through the portal as well, leaving Charlie and Brooke behind to face their doom alone.

Verminion and Barakkas warred like ancient gods of myth. Verminion slashed open Barakkas's shoulder with one gigantic claw. Barakkas roared, then grabbed the attacking claw at its root and snapped it off in a spray of ichor.

While Verminion howled in pain, Barakkas bent down and, using the two horns on the top of his head, flipped Verminion on to his back, exposing his underside. With one strong, swift motion, Barakkas used his good hand to drive Verminion's severed claw towards the translucent armour of his belly, aiming at the glowing red light of the bracer, which illuminated him from somewhere deep within.

The claw cracked the armour on Verminion's stomach with a sound like ice breaking underfoot, and as Verminion sliced Barakkas's face with his one good claw, Barrakas drove his fist deep into Verminion's innards, frantically fishing for the bracer he had lost.

Charlie, meanwhile, attacked the approaching Nethercreatures with desperate grace. His blazing blue rapier lopped off claws and eyes with astonishing precision. As he fought, one sharp realisation suddenly pierced through his battle rage.

They were going to die.

He could kill for days and never get to the end of the infinity of creatures that were rushing through dark and gloomy hallways to deliver their death. If only he could open a portal, *just a small one,* to escape through. But, as the Headmaster had said, even a Double-Threat couldn't open a portal and Banish at the same time, and if he stopped Banishing for even a second, they would eat him alive.

The beasts descended on the two of them like a hurricane – an infestation of darkness Charlie could not hope to repel. Swinging his rapier with amazing speed, he realised that in his attempt to rescue his parents, he had doomed them. Everyone else had been right and he had been wrong. He was a fool on a fool's errand and it had likely cost the lives of his only true friends and the parents who had always protected him. He didn't know what had happened to them down that dark tunnel, but he couldn't imagine they had survived the attack brought on by his incompetence. Surely they were dead now, dead because of him, and he was alone against the army of the Nether, an outcast in a world that hated him, with only a useless Facilitator by his side.

"I'm sorry," Brooke whispered as Charlie fought to protect her. "I wish I could help. If I hadn't lost the Gift, I could open a portal for us right now, but I *can't*." Tears of rage and helplessness poured down her cheeks. "I've never been any good," she said, sobbing, as her deepest fear was realised. "I'm a phoney and a failure. I'm useless and I always have been, and now we're going to die because of it!"

And that's when suddenly, amazingly, *a portal snapped open in front of them.*

Charlie's eyes went wide. "Did *you* do that?" he gasped.

"I... I guess I did," she said, astonished.

Far in the distance, Verminion howled in pain as Barakkas, wounded gravely, lifted his bracer from the stink of Verminion's swampy innards. It splashed crazy red light across the cavern walls, growing rapidly in size to fit his wrist.

"It's mine!" Barakkas yelled. "The bracer is mine once again!"

As the giant beast hooted in triumph, Charlie and Brooke leaped through the open gateway. The creatures of the Nether swarmed all over them then, but they were too late.

The portal – along with Charlie and the girl who had opened it – was gone.

CHAPTER SEVENTEEN
TRUTH AND CONSEQUENCES

After a brief stopover in the Nether, Charlie and Brooke leaped into the Nethermancy room in the heart of the Nightmare Academy.

"You did it," he said, turning to her.

"I guess I did," she replied. A sunny smile spread across her face. It was so warm and inviting that smile, that it made Charlie's heart ache. "I thought I had lost the Gift for ever, but I got it back."

"Just in time," Charlie said. "You were amazing."

"Thank you. So were you." She gave him a kiss then, quick and soft. It was his first one, and it was so sweet and perfect that Charlie wished it could go on for ever.

"My boy..." Olga said from somewhere behind him.

Charlie turned and saw his mother rushing towards him. She hugged him so tightly, he could barely breathe.

Charlie was shocked to discover how light she felt. She had grown so weak and thin in her imprisonment that it felt as though she might blow away in a strong breeze.

"Are you OK, Mum?" he asked.

"Oh, yes," she answered. "Now that I'm back with my boy." She licked her hand and began trying to wipe the volcanic soot from his face. "Look at you. You're a mess," she said. "An absolute fright."

Charlie's father joined them. "I thought we'd lost you, son," he said, his voice cracking. "We couldn't have abided it. It would have been... the end of me. Of both of us."

"I'm fine, Dad," Charlie said. "Really I am."

"The Benjamin men have faced their fears!" Barrington exclaimed. "And come out winners!"

Charlie smiled. "I guess so. It's so good to see you. I can't tell you how sorry I am that you both had to suffer like this."

"What doesn't kill us makes us stronger," Barrington said. "And your mother and I are now both very, *very* strong."

"And don't you *ever* blame yourself!" Olga scolded. "You hear me?"

"I hear you, Mum," Charlie said with a smile, then turned to Violet and Theodore. "How did you guys escape? I didn't think you had a chance."

"It's all her," Theodore said, pointing to Violet. "You

should have seen her. She was sick in there with that dagger. Sick! Fighting Netherstalkers – *whack, whack!*" He demonstrated by slashing a hand through the air. "Truly unbelievable. Definitely outrageous."

"And you should have seen the portal *he* made," Violet said. "There were creatures everywhere and he came in like Jordan at the buzzer and snapped open a gateway like you wouldn't believe."

"Aw, come on, it wasn't *that* amazing," Theodore replied, flushing with embarrassment but basking in the compliment none the less.

"Thank you both," Charlie said. "I can't tell you what it means to me."

"Ah, no worries," Theodore replied with a grin. "That's just the way we roll."

"Mr Benjamin!" a voice boomed from the far end of the Nethermancy room. Charlie turned as the Headmaster strode in, followed by Rex and Tabitha. "Good Lord, boy – you made it!"

Tabitha rushed over and gave Charlie a big hug. "We were so..." She struggled to find the words. *"You just need to be more careful!"* she said finally.

Rex clapped Charlie on the back. "Way to go, kid. How you pulled this off, I have no idea, but I am dang glad to see you."

"Same here," Charlie said, beaming. He turned to the Headmaster. "What did you end up doing with..."

"Director Drake?" she asked. "Why, he's right here. Come on in, Director."

The Director of the Nightmare Division entered the Nethermancy room and walked up to them. "Director Drake," the Headmaster said, "I'd like you to meet someone very special. This is Charlie Benjamin. He's quite Gifted."

"Pleased to meet you," Drake said, shaking Charlie's hand. "Work hard, study diligently and one day you may find yourself working for me in the Nightmare Division."

"Thank you, sir," Charlie said, then turned to the Headmaster. "The Hags, right?"

"Of course."

Rex sighed dramatically. "Those Hags turned my daddy into a liar, because he always said, 'Inside every beast lies a beauty', but there's nothing beautiful about those critters, inside or out."

Charlie laughed. "Your *father* said that?"

Rex nodded, grinning.

"Wait a minute," Charlie said, "if you remember your father, then that means..."

"That I got my folks back in the bargain, just like you."

"Really?"

"They're all right back in here where they belong," Rex replied, tapping his head with a forefinger. Charlie hugged him then, hugely relieved. "Hey, easy, kid," Rex said. "Let's not get *sentimental*."

The Headmaster turned to Charlie. "When you are ready, Mr Benjamin," she said, "we really should talk."

They stood on the deck of the pirate ship at the very top of the Nightmare Academy. The jungle spread out below them like a green velvet carpet. Brightly coloured birds flew through the trees, held aloft by the warm tropical breeze.

"So the Artefacts of the Nether are summoning devices," the Headmaster said, shaking her head gravely. "And you're certain that all four of the Named must be present together on Earth to use them to summon what they called 'the Fifth'?"

"That's what Barakkas and Verminion said," Charlie replied, nodding. "And they didn't know I was listening, so I think they were telling the truth."

"I wonder who or what this 'Fifth' is," the Headmaster said. "If it takes all four of the Named to bring it to Earth, it must be a very powerful creature indeed. We must do everything in our power to prevent it from being summoned by keeping the remaining two Named from crossing over to our world."

"Who are they?" Charlie asked. "The last two, I mean."

"Their names," the Headmaster replied, "are Slagguron and Tyrannus. Hopefully, you will never have the opportunity to make a personal introduction."

"You won't get any argument from me," Charlie said.

"The information you provided, though chilling, is *vital*, and I greatly appreciate your acquiring it for us."

"You're welcome."

"But I do *not* appreciate the lying and subterfuge you employed to make that happen," she continued darkly. "Though things turned out well, they could just as easily have gone very wrong."

"I know," Charlie said. "I see that now. Even though we succeeded, pretty much nothing went according to plan."

"It rarely does."

"I wanted to make Verminion and Barakkas think I was joining them, so that they would let Theodore and Violet take my parents away."

"And then you planned to escape with the bracer?"

Charlie nodded. "But Verminion sniffed out my plan."

"Deceivers are always excellent at knowing when they're being deceived," she said grimly.

"We survived," Charlie continued, "but *barely.*"

"Get used to it. My whole life has been a series of one 'barely' after another. When you left, the two Named were still fighting?"

Charlie nodded. "Yeah, they were tearing each other apart. The last thing I saw was Barakkas taking the bracer from Verminion's stomach. I'm not sure they could have survived."

"I see," the Headmaster said. "Well, whether they survive or not, you have clearly delivered them a serious blow. They will be in no condition to attack in the next month or even the next year. You have bought us some time."

"I guess... but Barakkas got the bracer."

"Yes, and that's unfortunate. But he would have got it eventually, and probably at the cost of many lives in the Nightmare Division." She was silent a moment. "All things considered," she said finally, "you and your friends succeeded quite remarkably, and the most amazing thing is that you did it all by yourselves."

"That's actually one thing I was wondering about," Charlie said. "I kept thinking that you guys might show up and, you know, save us or something."

"Did you?" she asked mildly.

"Yeah. At the end, when I was fighting half the lair, I

kept thinking – *hoping, I* guess – that you'd pop in and rescue me. Why didn't you?"

"Because I didn't know what your plan was. Had I arrived at the wrong time, I could have ruined everything. True?"

"True," Charlie conceded. "I just... I didn't figure you'd trust me like that."

She smiled warmly. "I had faith in you, Charlie, just like you asked me to."

"Thank you," Charlie said simply, then turned and stared out at the ocean. It seemed to go on for an eternity. "Where *are* we exactly? Here at the Nightmare Academy, I mean."

"Hidden," the Headmaster replied somewhat cryptically. "Just like your parents will have to be."

"*What?*"

"It's true, I'm afraid," she said. "When they have recovered from their ordeal, we will provide them with new names and identities and give them a fresh start – for their own protection."

"I don't understand! Can't they be protected *here*?" Charlie insisted. "There's nowhere safer. Even Barakkas couldn't attack us at the Academy."

"It is true that the Academy has its own *unique* form of defence against the creatures of the Nether." She lovingly rubbed the worn wooden railing of the pirate ship. "But that protection may not last for ever."

"What is it? How does it work?"

"That is a long story for another day," she replied. "I know you wish that your parents could remain here, but, as we have seen, they make you terribly vulnerable. Besides, the Academy itself is only a very small part of a very large island." She looked out across the broad expanse of jungle. Even though the sun was shining brightly on the treetops, Charlie couldn't see past them to the darkness below. "There are other dangers here," she said finally. "We are not alone."

Charlie was bursting with questions. What exactly *were* the Academy's defences? What was lurking in the jungle? Where would his parents be hidden? He wanted answers and he wanted them *now*, but the Headmaster didn't seem inclined to give him any. "When can I see my parents again?" he asked finally, hoping for an answer to that question at least.

"I'm not sure," the Headmaster replied. "They will need to remain hidden until we know the final fate of Verminion and Barakkas."

"I understand," Charlie said, and then he quickly turned away so that the Headmaster couldn't see the tears that were already beginning to sting his eyes.

Deep in the heart of Barakkas's and Verminion's lair, the two giants lay sprawled across the rough volcanic rock, which was now wet and sticky with their black blood. They were torn up almost beyond recognition. Netherstalkers attended them, stitching them back together, piece by ruined piece, using their tough silken webbing. The two Artefacts of the Nether glowed brilliantly in the darkness.

"Keep him alive," Barakkas gurgled, gesturing to Verminion. "All of the Four must be present or we will be unable to summon the Fifth."

"Yes, master," one of the Netherstalkers said.

Verminion lifted his bloodstained head and turned to Barakkas. "The boy... must pay," he gasped. "He must *die*."

"No," Barakkas replied. "He must *live*. And be made to suffer."

"Yes," Verminion said. "Good."

As lava flowed in glowing streams down the walls of the cavern, more Nethercreatures entered to attend to the crippled behemoths, using the full extent of their dark skills to coax the two beasts back from the brink of death.

Pinch sat alone on the rocks outside the cave that led to the Banishing arena. The salt spray from the crashing waves stung his face.

"I know what you must feel like."

Pinch turned to see Charlie standing there. "Do you?" he replied. "Do you really?"

They were silent a moment. Another wave tumbled in from the sea, leaving trails of lacy white bubbles on the sand. Gulls screeched overhead.

"If I could take it back," Pinch said softly, "I would. All of it."

"Me too," Charlie replied. "Back to before any of this ever happened. It's just... I've caused a lot of people a lot of pain."

"And you will cause more in the future," Pinch said, turning to him. "You can't control that – but you *can* control whether the pain you inflict comes to further the cause of something noble or something dark." He was silent a moment. "Don't do what I did," he said finally.

"I'll try," Charlie said. "It's just... it's not always easy to see which end is up, if you know what I mean."

"I'm afraid I do."

They sat in silence then as the sea foamed and churned at their feet. Charlie thought of the hundred and one ways that things could have, *should* have, gone horribly wrong.

It was only luck that had saved them this time.

Next time, luck might not be enough.

"Get over here, DT," a voice called from somewhere down the beach. It was Theodore, happily splashing in the surf with Violet.

"Yeah, the water's great!" she added with a gale of bright, carefree laughter.

It was music to Charlie's ears.

He walked towards them then, stopping only momentarily when he saw Brooke standing at the edge of the jungle by a grove of wild palms. She looked beautiful. He waved to her and she smiled and waved back. Seeing this, Geoff, her boyfriend, possessively slung his arm around her and steered her away from Charlie and into the darkness of the wild green jungle beyond.

"You coming?" Theodore yelled again.

"Coming," Charlie shouted back after Brooke was finally gone from view.

He turned then and ran down the warm sand towards his friends. Behind him, the Nightmare Academy rose into the sky, its catwalks swaying gently in the tropical breeze, its crazy quilt of cabins and sailing ships and hidden nooks and crannies just begging to be explored.

Charlie was glad he didn't have to do it alone.

DON'T DESPAIR – THE
FUN ISN'T OVER YET!

READ ON FOR A VERY EXCLUSIVE
SNEAK PREVIEW OF BOOK TWO IN THE
NIGHTMARE ACADEMY SERIES,

MONSTER REVENGE

A PORTAL SNAPPED open in the Headmaster's room and a large man stepped through. He was as straight and tall as the two-handed sword sheathed at his side.

"Dad!" Theodore exclaimed.

The man turned and silently inspected him. "Theodore," he said finally, without much emotion. "You've grown."

"Thanks!"

"Taller… but not wider. How do you expect to wield a weapon, skinny as you are?"

Theodore seemed to deflate. "But, Dad – you know I'm not a Banisher. I'm a Nethermancer, remember?"

"How could I forget?" He smiled grimly.

The way Theodore's father treated his son always

turned Charlie's stomach. Sure, Theodore wasn't a Banisher like the rest of the Dagget family, but he was an awesomely good Nethermancer. Didn't that count for something?

"What brings you to us, William?" the Headmaster asked.

"*General* Dagget, if you don't mind."

"General!" Theodore blurted. "No way! Congrats, Dad!"

"Thank you," William replied coolly.

"So how can we help you... General?" the Headmaster asked.

"Director Drake demands your presence immediately."

"Excellent. There is much I need to discuss with him. There is terrible trouble in the Nether."

"Not just you – *all* of you." William glanced around at the others in the room.

"Great," Rex grumbled. "Nothing I like more than getting marched over to the principal's office. He gonna paddle us? Make us stand in the corner with a dunce's cap on our heads?"

"You better hope that's *all* he does," William replied. "I'm not sure I've ever seen him this furious."

Day or night, the Nightmare Division was always the same. Windowless and sterile, it was an immensity of blinking, chirping electronics and it always seemed to be filled with adult Banishers and Nethermancers racing to repair a disaster or escort a Nethercreature to one of the hundreds of containment rooms in the secure facility.

"Let me do the talking," the Headmaster said as she steered them expertly through a maze of hallways. "I think we all know how difficult and unpredictable the Director can be."

"You can say that again," Theodore moaned. "That guy's a nut!"

Suddenly, a Class-3 Acidspitter herded by four Banishers broke free from its muzzle and sprayed acid at them as they passed. Without even breaking stride, the Headmaster casually opened a portal between the group and the creature, allowing the burning fluid to spray harmlessly into the Nether. Within moments, the Banishers subdued the monster and the Headmaster dismissed her portal.

Charlie marvelled, as he had so many times before, at how powerful and fast she was.

"Here we are," the Headmaster said as they stopped at the sleek steel door marked OFFICE OF THE DIRECTOR

– PRIVATE. "Remember, whatever happens, let me handle it."

The Director of the Nightmare Division was a tall man with steel-grey hair and grey eyes to match. In fact, he was so grey that he seemed to almost disappear into the metal walls of his chambers. His manicured fingers tapped incessantly on his chrome desktop as he stared at Charlie down his long, crooked nose.

"Charlie Benjamin…" he said slowly. "I *remember*."

Charlie's blood froze. "You remember?" he echoed uncertainly.

"Yes," the Director replied, savouring the word like a sweet that delivers new flavours the harder you suck it. "I remember how you brought Barakkas into our world, in spite of my dire warnings. I remember how I sentenced you to be Reduced so that you could never again harm us. I remember how your friends and teachers came to your aid against my direct orders. In short, I remember… everything."

Charlie felt light-headed. He desperately wanted to sit down, put his head between his knees, close his eyes and pretend this was all a bad dream – but he knew that was not an option.

Unfortunately, all of the things the Director said were true: he *had* allowed Barakkas to come to Earth and join Verminion. It had been accidental, of course. Charlie's untrained power was so strong that, under horrible stress, he had mistakenly opened a portal into the Inner Circle in the Nether and Barakkas had rushed through.

As a result, the Director had called for Charlie to be Reduced – a bland name for a barbaric surgical procedure that would have for ever stripped Charlie of the ability to portal or Banish. In fact, it had been done to Pinch as a child, leaving him bitter and powerless. The Headmaster, Rex and Tabitha had flatly refused to allow that to happen to Charlie, which placed them all squarely in the Director's crosshairs.

"You're probably wondering how I remember," the Director said, getting up from behind his desk and walking towards them. He ran his long fingers through his slicked back grey hair, releasing a waft of hair gel. "God knows you did everything on Heaven and Earth and elsewhere to make me forget."

And there it was finally.

The Hags, Charlie thought. *He knows about the Hags of the Void.*

"You must have thought you were so clever," the Director said, his eyes mere slits, "using the Queen of the

Hags to take away my memories of your crimes. How brilliant you all must have thought you were. How remarkably devious."

"What's he talking about?" Theodore whispered.

"I have no idea," Violet said with a shrug.

But I sure do, Charlie thought.

He hadn't been there when the Headmaster, Rex and Tabitha had kidnapped the Director and brought him to the Queen of the Hags, but he had seen what the foul beast could do. She flew towards you on her powerful, leathery wings, enfolded you in them and then, leaning back her green, scaly head, she snaked a shockingly long tongue through her forest of teeth and plunged it into your ear, where she sucked deeply of—

Your memories.

She ate them like chocolate buttons and, when she was done, you lost them for ever.

Except not this time.

The Hag Queen had taken all the Director's memories of Charlie and his friends... but somehow he had got them back.